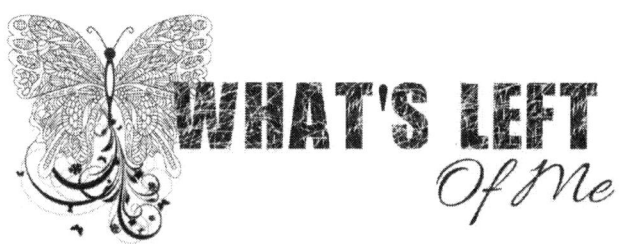

Finally Unbroken Series Book Two

MARIA MACDONALD

What's Left of Me
Finally Unbroken Series Book Two

Maria Macdonald

This book is a work of fiction. Any references to real events, real people, and real places are used fictitiously. Other names, characters, places and incidents are products of the Author's imagination and any resemblance to persons, living or dead, actual events, organisations or places is entirely coincidental.

All rights are reserved. This book is intended for the purchaser of this book ONLY. No part of this book may be reproduced or transmitted in any form or by any means, graphic, electronic, or mechanical, including photocopying, recording, taping, or by any information storage retrieval system, without the express written permission of the Author. All songs, song titles and lyrics contained in this book are the property of the respective songwriters and copyright holders.

ISBN-13: 978-1530958771
ISBN-10: 1530958776

Formatting by Swish Design & Editing
Editing by Swish Design & Editing
Cover design by Francessca's Romance Reviews
Cover image Copyright 2016

Copyright © 2016 Maria Macdonald
All rights reserved.

Dedication

For Laurie Breitsprecher.
You gave me your name.
But more…
You are the other half to my musical soul.

WHAT'S LEFT
Of Me

Prologue

Ruben

The bar feel's good, maybe I should live the rest of my days here.

None of it matters anymore anyway.

I stare at my empty glass. Beating everything back with alcohol is definitely the way forward. The smell that hangs in the air is stale, heavy with beer and sweat. It's a real bar, for men who want to forget. Men like me. That's why I want to stay here forever, even though everyone else has already left. This is the way of the world. In the end, I will always be on my own.

"Hey, buddy… Hey, you." The noise comes from behind the counter.

Moving my head causes the room to spin, but I can just about make out a blurred face.

"You need me to call someone?" the blur asks.

"Nobody to call," I slur as my head drops onto the counter top.

"Ruben… Ruben," the angelic voice wakes me. And for one, still, calm, warm minute, I forget everything and my world isn't tilted anymore. Then, as with every other time I've woken over the last three years, my peace is shattered when I remember and my world crumbles. It all filters into my mind at once, trying to suffocate me. What the memories forget, is that I want to be suffocated. As long as I'm here—alive, existing, barely—I'm lost to everyone, even myself. I don't have her, so there's nothing left of me. She took all the good I had with her. I tried to be a better person for Amanda, and everything I became was wrapped up in her, now I'm not sure who I am.

"Go away," I grunt.

"Come on, Ruben, they want to shut the bar." I recognize the voice now. *Laurie.* Fucking Laurie. Always trying to fix me.

"Leave. Now," I growl out.

"Dude, you have to leave. Don't make me call the cops."

What's Left of Me

I groan at the barman. Then pull my six-two frame from the stool and allow my eyes to cut across to Laurie Rosales.

"Hey Laurie, is it? This your man?" the bartender asks as I watch him leer at her.

She shakes her head while moving toward my swaying body.

"Can I have your number?" he asks hopefully.

She whispers a quiet, "No," followed by an apology. Which, in turn, makes him bang something and walk off. *Douche.* I stare at her for a moment, trying to see what he saw. With her long almost black hair, tanned skin and light blue eyes, she's probably every man's wet dream. *Not mine.*

"Would have thought you'd have something better to do on a Saturday night than be a babysitter." I stop talking and curl my lip. "Figures you'd be the one to try and save me. I can tell you now, ain't nothing left to save, darling."

"I'm just here to take you home, Ruben. I can't save you. That much I know." Her tone is soft, but her words are hard. Jagged around the edges. "You can't save someone who wants to drown, or you'll end up drowning with them." Turning, she walks away, stops, looks over her shoulder and says, "Are you coming? I'm not heaving your big frame, so you better hope those legs of yours still work." She glances down at my thighs with undiluted anger. It sears me to the bone. Then she walks away again, this time without a backward glance.

I'm jolted from my thoughts as we turn toward my house. I can't call it a home, I haven't had one of those since I was a child. As Laurie's car draws up outside, I close my eyes in frustration.

"Why the fuck did you call him?" I snap.

"Because I didn't know how bad you'd be. I can't look after you, it isn't r-really appropriate," she stutters and for the first time tonight, I feel a small frisson of guilt at the way I've behaved toward her. That gets easily washed away as she pulls into my drive, right next to Anabel's black Range Rover. Where an obviously annoyed Danny stands, arms crossed, one foot tucked behind the other ankle, leaning against the door, his eyes narrowed at me.

"I can't believe you fucking called him," I repeat myself still angry, even after her lame attempt at an explanation.

"I… it seemed… I mean… y-you—"

"Don't bother with your shitty excuses," I snarl while angling myself out of the car.

What's Left of Me

I hear her car door open and close softly behind me, but my eyes are narrowed on Danny's. Mirroring his scowl.

"Ruben... I'm sorry." Laurie's subdued voice carries over to me.

Without looking back, I snap, "Not interested. I won't be coming back to any of your do-gooder meetings anymore either..." I walk straight past Danny. "You can both fuck off, now you know I'm home."

Danny reaches out and grabs my arm, pulling me back. "Ruben, this shit has to stop," he growls out at me.

I look between him and Laurie. "What shit?"

"This shit! Getting drunk every fucking weekend. Needing one of us to save your ass."

"Fuck you, Danny. I never asked either of you to bail me out. How the fuck did they even know who to call?" I raise my voice.

"I put my number in your phone as your emergency contact." Laurie's voice is soft and calm like she's dealing with a feral animal.

"I gave Laurie my number and told her to call me if this happened again. After the last time..." Danny quietens down.

We're all silent. *I remember last time.* My ass was thrown in jail for drunk driving. The only saving grace was that the local sheriff knew Laurie. He called her to come bail me out. Still, if she thinks that means I owe her something, then she'll soon realize that she's made the wrong assumption.

I turn to her. "Go home. I'll take your number out of my cell. See you around." Moving back to the house, Danny grunts his disappointment at me. I don't give a shit.

"Ruben," he calls.

"What Danny? What? I'm home, I've sobered up," I say trying desperately to walk straight while blinking, attempting to clear the blur in my eyes. "Go home to your pregnant wife and your daughter." He doesn't move. *"Go!"* I shout.

"Fucking hell, Ruben. We're here, trying to help you," he shouts back.

"I didn't ask you to do dick. So as it seems to be such a hardship, here's me making it easier. Don't bother anymore." I turn away as my chest rises and falls rapidly, the anger is obvious with every biting word I speak.

"For fuck's sake, Ruben. It's been three fucking years since we lost her. *Three years!"*

I twist and move so quickly toward him that I'm sure any other man would back away, but not him, not Danny. As I stand nose to nose with my best friend, my voice quietens down. "Three years for you Danny. Three years for the world. When it's your world you lose… three years doesn't exist… three minutes don't exist. My world ends continuously. Every fucking time I open my eyes and remember. Every smell, every memory, every thought, and every time I look at the damn stars. Don't ever assume you know how I feel. You lost Anabel for years. You didn't lose her forever." I watch as pity fills his eyes. Then, because I can't take anymore, I back away quickly moving into the house and slamming the door, just trying to breathe.

Leaning forward, I brace myself with my palms on my knees, then shake it off, striding to the stairs. I need my bed. As I look up and out of the side window, the stars shine brightly.

"Don't judge me. I'm trying not to be a dick," I tell her—*my star.*

Getting no reply, I change course and go to the kitchen, grab a bottle of Jack from my stock and retrace my steps. This time I ignore the window, effectively blocking out the stars and enter my bedroom. Putting the bottle down to pull off my jeans, socks and shirt, before I sink into the bed and drown all over again. This time, Jack will be my friend. Jack will always be there for me.

Laurie

EIGHTEEN MONTHS LATER

"Thanks, Sarah, I'll take it from here," I tell my co-worker at the community center. The place that's been my home from home for the last five years, ever since I lost Larissa and Rocco.

"Sweet. I'm going to head off. I have Jim and the twins waiting for food. You know that house doesn't function without me," she says laughing and rolling her eyes. Like it's a hardship when everyone here knows how much she dotes on her family. Watching her walk out of the center, I pull my shoulders back and get ready to enter another new class. Walking in, I purposefully don't look at anyone. Always finding it easier to say the first few words without looking.

What's Left of Me

I've perfected my opening address since I started holding these classes about eighteen months ago. Unlike back then, I now start every new group with my story, to help them talk about theirs. Talking about my experience, usually helps them see that I do understand and that I can relate. I like to be the first to show my vulnerability, to show them I'm opening myself up to them, before asking that they do the same for me. Tying my jumper around my waist, I pace the circle of chairs, walking around the outside.

"I lost my sister and nephew five years ago. I took it hard, really hard…" I say offering a small smile to the group. "Grief is difficult. That part is obvious. Everyone knows it's not easy, even people who have never suffered through it. What's not always realized, sometimes even taken for granted… is the type of loss. I'll give you an example. Everyone in this circle has lost someone. Someone so important to them that they feel the need to come to a bereavement class. So, out of everyone in this building, *you* should know how hard it is. But even though we know that, I'd bet if I could get inside your minds, I'd find that at least one person out of the six of you heard me say… I lost my sister and nephew. And whether consciously or subconsciously, you thought, well that's not as bad as me… I lost my wife, husband, child, etc. It's a natural reaction, even if it's not a fair one."

I stop speaking and swallow, knowing the hard part is coming. "If I then went on to say… my sister was my twin. She was my world. She had my nephew Rocco when she was seventeen. Her then boyfriend left, and our parents disowned her. I took her side, left when they kicked her out. We moved a lot, and at seventeen, we weren't supposed to be in the big wide world on our own. Not yet, especially when one of us was pregnant. As Larissa got bigger, I picked up whatever jobs I could. I've been a checkout girl, right through to a stripper…" as I hear them gasp, I smile.

"I was eighteen when I had to strip. Still, I have no regrets, it was good money. Rocco needed diapers and formula, and I'd pretty much do anything for that kid."

I stop pacing and hang my head for a second. "Larissa began having problems. She'd fall for no reason. It started happening a lot, then it escalated. She started having trouble getting up when she was lying down, and she was having lots of muscle pain and stiffness. It was hard to find out the cause because even at eighteen, we didn't have healthcare insurance. She was eventually diagnosed with Muscular Dystrophy. It started affecting her pretty badly. It would've been easier on her if we could've gotten the treatment she needed. But all the money I made went on Rocco, making sure that little boy got everything *he* needed, but forgetting in the process that what he needed most was his mother."

I clench my teeth as my tummy flutters. Second guessing myself, my actions, and wishing I'd made different choices. Maybe if I'd focused more on getting her the help she required, we wouldn't have been in the car that day. I give my head a little shake, trying to push out the questions I've asked myself a million times since that fateful day, and still not having the answers. I don't look to the group, knowing their attention is solely on me. Instead, I pull myself together and continue the story.

"She got depressed and I would be out all day, trying to work, to get money and providing, so Rocco could eat, and every other night we too were able to eat. She was stuck at home, with her beautiful son. But he was a baby, he needed everything doing for him and eventually, she couldn't do it anymore. Physically it was too difficult, and she was getting worse, rapidly. I started spending more time at home, which meant less money for us, but I got to look after Rocco. From nearly his birth, until he died, I was that kid's mom. I bathed him, fed him, and went to his soccer games. *Loved him*.

"Five years ago, Rocco was eight and Larissa twenty-five. We were getting a ride in a neighbor's car to the clinic for Larissa. She wasn't doing too well. Our neighbor was a lovely gentleman, he was around sixty. His wife had died a few years before, so he was on his own. We used to bundle together, like a makeshift family. He'd take us to appointments, and we had him over most nights for charades. He would often bring food, which I'd cook for all of us. I hated the thought of him being across the hall all alone when he could spend some time with us. That Monday was no different to countless others over the years. Except it was. That Monday changed my whole life."

I stop talking, biting my lip instead. The next part is always the hardest. The emotion rolls through my chest, stopping at my heart which is now thumping hard and fast. And I know if I don't just breathe, I'll break down in the middle of class. It's happened before and it wasn't pretty. These people need to see someone stronger, someone who's survived death and loss the same way that they have, or at the very least, to show them that they can. They don't need to know I'm still broken, hollow, and that sometimes everything just seems pointless. In truth, the people here, they're what keep me going. To know there's a small chance I can help someone else, makes me feel like my life is worth something, and that's all I have to stop me from giving up some days. I turn to the circle of faces, not really seeing any of them, everything's a blur at this point.

What's Left of Me

Sucking in a breath I climb my personal mountain. *Again.* "Mr. Kendall had a heart attack on the way to the hospital. We crashed. Larissa died on impact. Mr. Kendall had already died from the heart attack, well… that was what they told me later. I came out practically unscathed, just a few cuts and bruises. And Rocco…" I shake my head sadly, "…he survived, in hospital, for three days. He fought, with everything his little body had to try and survive. Ultimately, he couldn't win. He didn't win. He was bleeding internally, and so never woke up. But I swear… *I swear* he squeezed my fingers right before he passed."

I wipe away the single tear that I allow out of my eye, as I remember them, him. "I miss them all. But Rocco… he was like my child. And I know nothing will ever fill the hole in me. The one that he left. I could meet someone, get married, and have my own children. Still, nothing will ever take his place. He'd be thirteen now. Probably cheeky…" I stop and chuckle to myself, imagining the little man he would have turned into.

"Sometimes I see him, in the people I pass in the street, wondering what he'd look like. How tall he'd be. I also wonder if Larissa would still be with us. She was deteriorating, so there's no saying. But Rocco was only eight… eight years old…" I still and breathe deeply, controlling, calming, "…so when I say I lost my sister and my nephew, there's more to it than what probably meets the eye. We all have our own loss, no *one* person is worse than the next. It took three years for me to tell anyone my story. Another six months to be able to bring the story into these groups. In the last eighteen months, I've held a group like this nine times. A new one every two months. I can safely say, on my experience so far, it never gets any easier."

I look at my hands which are now shaking. "Each time I feel like my heart is being ripped out. But, I'm going to tell you something else. At the same time the pain is there, I can feel the healing that's taking place too. Who knows, maybe in another eighteen months it'll feel easier telling my story. What I do know is that I have to keep trying, and maybe I'll always be trying. I won't ever stop, though. Because I knew a little boy, one that would've loved to live his life, but had it taken away too soon. What am I showing him if I waste my existence? I'm saying it doesn't matter. The *he* didn't matter. After all, if I don't care about my own survival, then why would I care about any of it? I might as well be telling him that it doesn't matter that he died because life isn't worth living. Personally, I want to know, that if he's looking down at me he'd be proud. Not ashamed."

I finish the introduction to my bereavement class and take a few moments, for myself and for everyone else, to hopefully allow my words to sink in. Then, slowly, I raise my head and look at each of them, one by one. Some are crying, some remain impassive. The one thing they have in common is the pain in all their eyes. Then, the last person makes me jolt.

Ruben Asher.

It's a face I haven't seen for eighteen months. He's the reason I changed these meetings. He's the one I couldn't reach. And he's staring at me like he finally wants me to save him.

Chapter Two

Ruben

I watch her walking back and forth. Can't take my damn eyes off her. When I last saw Laurie all those months ago, she was a different person. Confident, but completely closed off. I never saw her suffering, she kept it hidden well. Now she's raw. I'm not surprised I didn't see it before. Although I didn't care to look back then, only coming to the bereavement group because Anabel strong-armed me into it, saying some shit about it being what Amanda would want. I didn't want to know about Laurie's pain. *Fuck, I didn't care about my own pain.* Using alcohol to keep me numb for the most part, but still wanting to *feel* the torment. No. *Needing* to feel it. Figuring, if Amanda can be dead then I should, at least, be able to hold onto the agony of her loss. I didn't want to forget. The pain helped me to always remember.

Now, watching Laurie, it's the first time I've ever really seen her. Before, in the other group I attended, she kept it hidden well by wearing a mask. I wasn't looking too hard, consumed in my own grief, but even so I could still see that she was hiding behind it. Now she's ripped wide open, it's like the loss is fresh. And I just can't seem to look away.

It's been five years since I lost Amanda. I have good days and bad days. I'm still fighting every damn day, just to live a little. I spiraled, and was completely out of control, nearly killing myself in the process. Danny and Anabel stepped in, making me go to rehab. It was the best thing they could have ever done for me, but I hated them for it. Since coming out of rehab, I've been to a few meetings. I started with the alcoholics group. Getting clean from the alcohol was something that I desperately needed. But I can't lie and say there aren't days I just want to reach for the bottle. Still, I'm working on it. Having come out on this side, I'm only just now starting to see clearly. I wish Amanda were still alive. It constantly hurts, but I don't feel like I'm going to drown all of the time. Sometimes, though… sometimes I could use a fucking motorboat to pull me out from the all-consuming waves that engulf me.

"So, I'm going to go around the group. If you could give your names, I'd appreciate it. If you want to add a bit about yourself, or your loss, then please do," Laurie tells us all. She moves, sitting in the empty chair, completing the circle and she looks to her left. The girl who sits there can't be more than twenty-two.

"H-Hi, I'm Shana. I'm twenty-three. Three months ago I lost my mom." She smiles sadly at Laurie but doesn't say any more.

"Hi Shana, welcome to the group," Laurie returns, then looks to the next person. This time, it's an older man, about fifty. He grabs hold of Shana's hand and smiles the same sad smile as her.

"I'm Chris, Shana's pop. Three months ago I lost my wife, Veronica." His voice breaks at the end and Shana shoves her face into her pop's chest.

"Hey Chris, thanks for joining us," Laurie tells him, her voice is raspy and warm. She shows the emotion she feels, letting them know that she understands their sorrow.

Next, we move onto the woman who sits to my left. She's around thirty, well dressed and obviously has money if her designer clothes are anything to go by.

"I'm Estelle. Last week my husband died. I'm here because I'm devastated," she says, matter-of-factly. I can see it takes the whole group aback slightly. Laurie welcomes her, and I wonder what her story is. At that thought, she glances up to me, obviously not having seen me before. She smiles, it's a flirty smile, and she makes me feel uncomfortable.

Laurie interrupts with a cough.

I look back and realize it's my turn. "Oh hey, I'm Ruben. Thirty-Seven." I add my age as an afterthought. Not really wanting to say anything else. Laurie holds my eyes for a second, offers me a sad smile, then nods.

"Hey Ruben, thanks for being here," she murmurs.

Before she can look to the last person, the dude on my right gets up and rushes out.

Calmly Laurie stands. "Sorry everyone. Please, just give me a moment, okay?" She smiles and walks out.

Looking around the group and not knowing what to do. But feeling—not for the first time—
like it's all a lie. That none of this crap is going to ever help me. I'm always going to be damaged and just like Laurie, I'll be looking for someone to save me for the rest of my life. Glancing around at everyone, I do the same as the other guy. Standing, I grab my jacket, throwing it on as I move to the exit. Once I'm outside, I breathe, leaning against the wall. Fresh air enters my lungs and I exhale, trying to regain my composure.

"Ruben?" The angelic voice makes me close my eyes, hoping I haven't just been caught running away. I open them and look to my right. The entrance to the community center is only a few feet away. "I came outside after that guy, but he's gone. You're leaving, too?" Laurie asks even though it's obvious.

"Just needed some fresh air," I lie.

"Can I ask you a favor?" she ask biting her lip. I nod. "Can you hang around? There's a coffee room out back. Stay, please, at the end of the hour I'll come find you. Of course, if you don't want to stay, then go. There's no pressure," she tells me, then slips in through the emergency exit I just exited closing the doors behind her.

I don't move. Just breathing seems to scar my lungs. My minds conflicted. I'm so used to the pain. Since I came out of rehab, since it took the edge off, it's made me start to face the things I've avoided before. Even the consideration of trying to heal has never been an option for me.

What if I get better?

What if I try and succeed?

I'm not sure if I know how to be whole anymore. I've lived broken for so long, I'm not sure I can live any other way. It's been a worthless life for the last few years. If it weren't for Danny, taking control of my company, I'm pretty sure I wouldn't still be a wealthy businessman either. I lack interest in that side of my life, but I'm trying. I'm still half the man I want to be. I never really lived a full life until I made my way back to my hometown until Amanda came back into my world. I had two glorious months of living full and complete. Being whole. I know how it feels now. Knowing you have to live forever with that loss, not just of her, but of yourself, is a pretty big fucking hit. I'm so scared that if I change, if I heal, if I start leading a life worth living, I'll forget Amanda and I'll sully her memory.

No. I need to remember the pain.

Pushing off the wall, I walk away from my chance at absolution. I don't deserve to live happily. I couldn't save Amanda. She doesn't get to be by my side. I only ever wanted to find my other half, the one who would make me a better man. I remember my mom telling me that there was one person who was our perfect fit. I lost mine. But my heart was torn in two in the process. One side is scared that this is all I have to look forward to for the rest of my days. The other half is telling me I'm a selfish prick for even thinking that way, and that I should be glad I got to have two months with my perfect person.

Stopping to look up, my feet have automatically brought me to the nearest bar. Checking my watch, I see it's opening time. I hear the doors unlock, then swing open. The man on the other side stands looking at me. "In or out?" he questions after I stare at him unmoving.

"In," I reply and enter the first bar I've been in for over twelve months.

Chapter Three

Laurie

"Hey," I greet Amber while closing the door with my foot. My hands full with grocery bags and the key I used to open the door. "A little help," I mutter. She doesn't move, and it's not until I walk past her on my way to the kitchen that I realize she hasn't heard me.

Pulling her earphones out of her ears, she rushes to me. "Shit, sorry, I didn't hear you."

"Language," I scold.

She smirks and starts rifling through the paper bags, looking to see what she can inhale. At eighteen, she's just about to go off to college with a full scholarship in medicine.

"Ooo donuts," she screeches, pulling her hand out, which is attached to some sugary goodness while her other hand delves in tagging another one.

I roll my eyes. "Don't spoil your dinner. It's noodles," I grumble.

"Never." She giggles then smirks, falling back onto the couch and shoving a whole donut into her mouth, before turning back to her book. She pops her earphones in and the iPod starts back up, I can hear the screaming rock from across the room.

Smiling, I unpack the rest of the food. For me, money is still a problem, Amber only has that iPod as a gift from Sarah. I glance around the kitchen at the beige tiles and the battered brown worktops. The kitchen is really just an extension of our living room, separated by a breakfast bar. People do that on purpose now, have their kitchen and living area separated by just a countertop like I have. But usually, it's a huge space, with a modern design and new appliances. My apartment was designed like this. The developers trying to fit as many apartments into as small a space as possible. I moved in here four years ago.

After losing Larissa and Rocco, I pooled together what little money I could afford for their funerals, but it still wasn't enough. I needed to use the rent money too. It was one too many times for the landlord, so needless to say, he kicked me out and I headed over to a shelter. Told him I'd be back for my things, but when I arrived back the next day, I found what remained of our belongings on the street. I was left with nothing. When I say nothing, I mean it in the literal sense. Anything worth something was stolen. I had the clothes I was wearing. And after rifling through what I was able to salvage—and carry in a bag on my back—I got a few clothes, a bag to put them in, a photo album and Rocco's favorite teddy.

The first shelter I went to pointed me in the direction of the community center. Somewhere that helps people get back on their feet, amongst other things. I was one of the people they helped. In a way, I still am. The bereavement course I run helps me as much as them. I moved from shelter to shelter for about a year. Through that time, I'd been cleaning the center. It paid nothing really, but I was used to nothing and was good at budgeting. As soon as I could, I found this place. It's no palace, but I keep it clean and tidy, and when I have the money, warm. It only has one bedroom and one bathroom, but I survive. *We survive*.

Amber came to the community center two years ago. She was sixteen, her mom had just died. Drugs. That life, the life of a drug addict, was threatening to take her over too. After she came to my class, I got to know her and spent some time with her outside of the community center. Not exactly the way they like things to run over there, but I was never able to keep myself emotionally distant from people, so I offered her my couch. It's been hers ever since. Amber gave me something when she moved in here. Something I needed desperately, something I craved, even though I didn't realize it back then. Amber gave me family again. Once I got her back into the local public school, she proved just how studious she was. Having good grades has gotten her to where she's going, and I couldn't be prouder. Now I have her for only another two months before she leaves, spreads her wings, and I'm once again on my own.

I sit next to her, tucking my legs under my butt and switch on the cheap, small television. After assessing that, as per usual, there's nothing worth watching, I pull an old magazine that I swiped from the community center out of my bag and flick it open.

"You okay?" Amber mutters beside me.

"What? Yeah. Why?" I reply, looking up at her.

"Because you've had that open on the same page for the last fifteen minutes. I know you read slowly, but these pages just have photos of badly dressed celebs. There's nothing worth fifteen minutes of time in there," she tells me, pointing to the magazine with a smirk.

"Oh…" I shake my head, "…I guess I was just thinking about someone."

"Who?" she immediately asks.

I sigh. Amber was around the last time Ruben was, and she knows the full weight of him being back. "Ruben."

"What? Why would you be thinking about him? And after all this time," Amber snaps, jumping up from her seat, sending her books flying.

"Calm down. He's gone again," I tell her.

"What?" she shrieks.

"He came to the start of my new course today. But when I was doing the introductions, there was another guy who ran out. So I followed the guy, looked wherever I could inside then ran outside. When I did, Ruben was there, standing against the wall and looking freaked. He'd obviously escaped the meeting the minute I'd gone after the other guy. I knew he wasn't about to go back in. I asked him to meet me in the coffee room once the session was over. I told him there was no pressure. When I went there after, he wasn't there. Stupid really." I sigh pulling my legs up and wrapping my arms around myself in a protective ball. "I knew he was a flight risk." I laugh softly.

"I can't flipping believe this!" Amber complains starting to pace. "He basically used you as a leaning post for four months. You saved him from jail, stopped him from doing countless stupid things. You helped him at the drop of a hat. Then, the one time you call his best friend, knowing he needed someone else to step in, and he cut you off. You were a wreck after that. Do you even remember, Laurie?" Amber shouts, flinging her arms about in an eighteen-year-old girl way.

I nod. I do remember. I remember feeling his pain as though it were my own. Feeling like I was falling. My own grief not enough, I was being dragged down by his too. He was the one I could never save, no matter how hard I tried. I gave more to him than anyone else. I'm not sure at what point I realized that my feelings ran deeper than they should. But Ruben was drowning, he couldn't see anything but pain and destruction. No matter what I did, it wasn't me that was supposed to heal him. Before him, I'd gone from all-encompassing pain and grief to dealing with things in a constructive way. Ruben Asher came crashing into my life, never offering me anything. I was supposed to be there to help him, and all I did was allow myself to fall for someone unattainable. I ended up being pulled back into the pit of despair for a while.

It wasn't his fault. It was mine. I allowed myself to think I could be enough. He'll never get over his ghosts. It's taken me a long time to realize that. He made me face up to some of my own pain. Anguish and blame, that I had covered over for so long, but never fixed. He made me change how I viewed the course my life ran. How I helped people. After

Ruben, I tried to stay detached from people. Like I'm supposed to. Danny and Anabel tried to keep in contact with me, but I cut them off. It was easier that way. I move through each day the same way now. If it weren't for Amber, my life would be gray.

"I remember," I tell her.

She comes to sit back next to me. "I'm sorry that I shouted. I just don't want you to get so low again. He did that, even if he wasn't aware. I'm leaving soon. That scares me enough."

"You'll be fine," I tell her wrapping my arm around her shoulders and pulling her close.

"It's not me I'm worried about Laurie."

I swallow and manage a small nod. "If we all have one person meant for us, then I'm pretty sure he was mine. Even if only from a distance. The problem is his person wasn't, and never will be, me. So I know I can't let myself fall down that rabbit hole again. But I won't turn him away Amber. Maybe this time, if I'm able to help him, it might give me some closure," I tell her on a squeeze.

"Hmm. You need to do what's best. Just do me a favor," she says.

"Anything honey," I reply looking down at her worried face.

"Just be careful," she whispers.

"I will." My reply is solid, I just wish everything else was.

Chapter Four

Ruben

"Ruben?" Anabel's surprised voice warms me from down the phone line.

"Anabel. It's good to speak to you, babe."

"Are you okay?" I know she's surprised to hear from me, even if I can't see her face. When I need something, or when I call to check in or catch up, it's always through Danny. Although, with her appeasing voice, I'm thinking I should make more time for chats with her.

"I'm downtown. On 54th Street. At Famous Eds," I tell her and wait.

"What! Ruben, I thought you'd gotten stronger. If you were still struggling, you should've stayed at our place for longer. You know you're always welcome here, with us. Why did you have to go to a bar the first week you move back into your apartment?" She's annoyed, I can hear it, but she's not shouting at me. No. It's worse than that. It's disappointment I hear in her tone.

"Anabel. I haven't had a drink," I tell her soberly.

"W-what? Really?" she asks.

"Yeah. I tried something. Didn't work out. Had a hard time and ended up here. I pulled my shit together at the last minute and ordered a coke. But Anabel, I could use a weekend at your place. Can I come up?" I ask.

"Of course! What did I just say to you, Asher?"

She used my surname, she only does that when she's pissed.

I bite the inside of my mouth, so I don't chuckle.

"You know Danny's away this weekend, though, right?" she asks.

"Yeah. I figured you could use some company. With two girls and being pregnant and all." I chuckle now.

"I'm perfectly capable, I'm not an invalid you know!" she snaps and I chuckle some more, before becoming serious.

"Anabel. I could use some time with *you* actually. I want to talk through some issues. Amanda related." I manage to force the words out.

"Oh. Of course. Come down tonight, okay? I'll make mac and cheese," she tells me and I can almost hear my stomach growl. Anabel's mac and cheese is fucking amazing.

"Be there in a couple of hours, babe. I'll call Danny, give him the heads up too," I say to her before disconnecting. I pull my hand down my face, feeling it in my gut. For once I'm doing the right thing. I'm trying to be better… for myself this time. With just that thought, a weight lifts and I know I'm going to feel complete again.

A few hours later, I'm at Danny's. I've spent the last hour chucking the girls around and chasing them through the rooms. Danny better hope this next baby is a little dude because these women know how to wrap a guy around their finger. He's fucked. I stopped playing when Anabel shouted at me. Something about it being their bath and bedtime, and they didn't need to be riled up. I couldn't help smirking, which didn't help the situation.

Making my way outside, grabbing a bottle of water as I go, Anabel has a whole relaxation area set up out here. Soft outdoor sofas surround a low table, there's decking to one side with a huge grill and counter next to it. A fridge sits underneath with drinks. It only has soda and bottles of water in there, though. Ever since I came out of rehab, Danny and Anabel have lived without alcohol too. They try to tell me it's because she's pregnant, but even when she wasn't, they cleared every bit of my poison from their lives. It's an act I'm immensely grateful for. Across to the far side of the garden is a small wall which has a gate, which stops anyone from going in. Behind that wall is a telescope. Also, behind that wall, is something I try to avoid when I visit. I sink into the sofa, not quite able to pull my eyes from the stars.

"It's peaceful out here tonight. Don't you think?" Anabel asks, settling herself next to me. I say nothing and just nod my response. "Do you still talk to her?" she asks, diving right in. Sometimes I think Anabel knows me better than Danny. It might be the maternal female in her, or it could be that she was Amanda's best friend. Soul mates they used to call themselves. If that's true, then Anabel knows Amanda's soul like no other, which would explain how she can know me so well.

"Yeah." My answer is short.

"Every day?" she shoots back.

I swallow, not wanting to answer truthfully, but knowing I have to. "No. Do you?"

"Yeah." She sighs and I hang my head. "It's okay, you know."

"What?" I say to my boots.

"Not talking to her every day." I don't answer, as I'm not sure I agree. "You know, we talked, Amanda and me about you before she died. I've told you before. She didn't want you stuck in the past. She wanted you to have a future. Think, if it were the other way around, you wouldn't want her to live like this, right?"

"I'm not stuck in the past, I—"

"Bullshit," she snaps jumping up. Anabel rarely uses profanities, so when she does, people take notice. My body jerks at her angry tone, but I don't move. "Don't try and kid a fucking kidder. I've lived in my past for over ten years, Ruben. *Ten fucking years!* Now that's exactly what you're doing. Blaming everything else for the reason you're the way you are. Telling yourself everything is good because you gave up drinking. But that's not everything, it's not the only demon you have. If you continue to live like this, a half existence, then you might as well still be drinking. At least then, you'd be numb, and maybe you'd move on to the next life sooner. That's what you want isn't it? To die? To be one of the stars? Up there next to her?"

She stands in front of me panting, and I stare up at her. Poking her finger in my face, she continues tearing me a new one. "Because if it's not, then you need to pull your head out of your ass and start rebuilding your life. Have fun, go back to work. *Love someone new*." My mouth drops open at the last statement. "What? You think you should be single forever? You think that's what she'd want?"

"No. It's not that," I reply, my voice scratchy.

"Then what?"

I know I need to be honest, and that I came here to Anabel for a reason. "I'm not sure I can be with someone new."

"Of course, you can. It just needs to be the right person." Her words have become soft, and my mind jumps to a pretty tanned face, with bright blue eyes and shiny dark hair. I shake my head, trying to rid myself of Laurie's image.

"I went back to the community center and saw Laurie." Internally, I junk punch myself. Not sure when my mouth stopped following orders and ran away with itself.

Anabel smirks. "How is she?" she asks, sitting back down next to me.

"I-I don't know, I walked out," I admit.

"What? Why?" she questions and I shake my head, not really sure why I do anything anymore. "Are you going back?"

"I'm not sure," I reply. She opens her mouth to speak, but I get there first. "Listen. I'm not trying to be awkward. I'm just not convinced that those types of groups are any good for me," I explain.

"Well, can't you ask her for some one-on-one help?"

I think back to Laurie's offer, to meet me in the coffee room. Maybe she was going to extend her help to outside of the course, but I didn't give her the chance.

"I feel like everything I do is a betrayal of Amanda," I say the words on an exhale, it's a release, finally saying the truth out loud.

"Why would you ever think that?" Anabel asks, leaning forward and taking my hand.

"Because I'm alive and she's not. Because I get to carry on. Because I told her, I'd only ever love her," I say the last part and my shoulders sag.

"Hey…" Anabel nudges my arm and I look back to her, "…you said that to her and what did she say back?" My body stills at her question and I turn my head away. "Tell me," she demands.

Growling, I reply, "She said I was a douche." Anabel snorts with laughter. "She said that I have a lot of love to give. That I proved myself to be an amazing boyfriend. She said—"

"What?" Anabel encourages.

"She said I need to be a father someday. That I'd be awesome at it, but that I had to be one hundred percent in love with the woman who was to carry my children. Because it was only fair that every child should have the best start possible. Being in love with their mom was a must. Amanda said I'd had a couple of months with her, the fact that she was..." I swallow back the boulder edging its way up my throat, "...the fact that she was dying made me feel more. For the record, I don't see how that's fucking possible."

"What else?" Anabel asks and I wonder how the fuck she knows that more was said.

"She told me that I should love again. Find someone special, and love her like I'd never loved anyone. Not even her. Amanda said she taught me how to love, and she'd always be proud of being able to give that to me. But now... it was my time to go find a woman who was everything I need." I stop talking and glance to the stars. "It's all fucking female bullshit anyway."

Anabel stands up. "I'm going to bed. The kids, plus being pregnant make me sleepy."

I nod but say nothing else. Unsure what to say, since the conversation has changed so dramatically with no warning.

She starts to walk away then stops. "For what it's worth, Ruben. Female bullshit or not, I agree with her. I did then, and now she's gone... I still agree. You just need to let everything go. She's gone, but she was always wise. What she said, those were words from her heart. She said them because once she was gone she wanted you to be free. Allow yourself to be free. If you need answers, do what I do. Talk to the stars, ask her for the rain." She smiles at me before walking away.

It's been years since I've spoken to the stars, and I'm not about to start now. I just sit and stare at nothing, wanting to think about Amanda. But the images in my mind keep changing back and forth from her to Laurie. It's not what I want. I don't want to forget Amanda. Shaking my head, I stand and turn to face the house. Everything's in darkness now, except one outside light. As I walk back, I feel the first few drops of rain and it feels like burning against my skin.

Chapter Five

Laurie

The tap on my shoulder makes me jump. Spinning around I see Sarah's mouth moving, but with Amber's iPod in my ears and Linkin Park blaring, I have no idea what she's saying. I put the bucket and cloth down and pull my earphones out.

"Sorry, what did you say?" I ask.

"There's a guy downstairs for you," she tells me. I notice her cheeks are red and she's puffing slightly, with a sheen of sweat across her brow she's obviously run up the stairs at pace.

I wonder what the rush was for?

"Who?" I ask confused. I'm not expecting anyone. I'm *never* expecting anyone unless it's Amber, but she doesn't introduce herself seeing as she knows everyone here. I rarely have any of the people from my sessions come visit me outside of the weekly meetings.

"I have no idea. But girl, let me tell you, I wish I did. That fine ass down there's looking like he needs some good lovin'. All broody, sexy and chiseled. Oh my God! I ain't never seen a man look like that, except on the covers of magazines. And he smells so damn good, too," she tells me fanning herself.

"I'm sure Jim would be delighted to hear you say all that," I reply with a smirk.

"Pfft. Jim can have his free pass with *Halle Berry* if I can have a pass with that tall glass of hot spicy rum down there." I laugh at her, then pull my gloves off, leaving them next to the cleaning stuff. "I'll carry on with these windows until you're done," Sarah tells me before I walk away.

"You don't have to do that," I reply.

"Oh, I know, but this way I'll be the first to get all the gossip about sex on a stick downstairs."

"Can you possibly come up with anything to give *more* of an impression you think the guy downstairs is hot?" I ask smirking.

"Yeah. But I want to know what the deal is. So get and find out. Go on, get." She shoos me away and I grin.

What's Left of Me

Heading downstairs, when I round the last set of stairs, I see him. *Ruben Asher.* His back is toward me, his body strung tight. I'd know that man anywhere.

"Ruben." I catch my breath, almost unaware that the word was going to pop out of my mouth.

His body jolts, like he forgot what he was here for and that he asked to see me. He turns to look at me, his face blank and his chiseled jaw—that Sarah was talking about only moments before—is set. The short hairs across the lower half of his face, along with the dark blond hair that curls at his neck, give him the rugged look. He pins me with his steely gray eyes as I come to a stop at the bottom of the stairs.

"Laurie." My name on his lips sounds like a promise. I'm just not sure what he's promising me. "I'm sorry if I'm interrupting."

I don't answer him, waiting to see what he'll say. We stand in this weird trance, taking in every detail about each other. Like we're breathing each other in, like that will make us understand what the other wants, or what the other needs. We're in a bubble. In another existence to everyone else, a little ball of glass, until someone walks in the front door and that ball shatters. It's a sharp reminder not to allow myself to get carried away.

"This was probably not a good idea anyway," he says, before turning to walk away. *Again.*

"What did you come here for?" I ask quickly, eagerly.

His stride stops and he drops his head. "I'm not really sure. Nothing. Everything." I can hear the pain in every word.

"Look, I'm finished working now," I lie. "Give me two minutes to grab my purse and we can take a walk if you want?" He doesn't say anything, just nods. "Okay, I'll be back. Don't leave this time. Please," I whisper but don't wait for his reply. Instead, turning and scrambling up the stairs.

"Tell me everything," Sarah demands as I arrive back to my station.

"I can't, he's here, but he's not really. Sorry, I can't explain right now. I'm going to go for a walk with him. If I don't get down there now, I think he might run, he's done it before." I stop and shake my head absentmindedly. "He's a flight risk," I mutter. Sarah looks at me like I'm crazy. Having never told her about Ruben it's not surprising she'd think that. "Listen, if you could put this stuff away for me, I'll finish the cleaning later. Pretty please?" I almost beg, desperate to get back downstairs before he leaves. Sarah just nods her head confused. I grab her hands in mine, giving them a squeeze, then run toward the stairs.

"I want all those details later," she shouts after me.

What's Left of Me

I'm almost shocked when I get to the bottom and Ruben's still there, waiting for me. "Come on," I tell him opening the door.

"Do you want a coat? It's cold out."

I look down at my body. "I-I don't have a coat," I reply, embarrassed.

"You left it at home?" he asks.

I shrug, not wanting to go down this route. I rarely tell anyone outside of my group anything about me. Sarah and Derick–my managers–are the only people who really know my situation. Ruben doesn't say anything and I don't look at his face, not wanting to read what he's thinking.

"You want to grab a coffee?" he asks and I open my mouth, not sure how to say no when he continues, "My treat. I came to you, the least I can do is buy you a coffee." I nod my head and hope like hell he doesn't see me as a charity case. I'm not too proud, if I were I'd be dead by now. At the same time, I don't want to seem like I mooch off people. It's a fine line to tread, and I'm constantly balancing trying to keep control.

Ruben leads us into a local coffee house and guides me to a table. "What do you want?" he asks as I take my seat.

"Just a flat white please." Nodding, he moves to the counter.

Looking around the place, I see there are only a few customers apart from us. All of them look like they're aren't there through choice, but trying to stay out of the cold. Each one of them huddled around a cup like it's going to keep them from their reality. I know that look, I've lived that look.

"Here," Ruben says, placing a cup in front of me.

I take in his clothes. Despite the rugged look, it's obvious his clothes are designer. Sharp, dry clean only type of material. He's out of place here. He always was.

"I know you don't live around here, you weren't just passing. So can I ask—"

Before I finish his eyes move from his cup to meet mine and he finishes my sentence. "What I'm doing here?" I nod but say nothing. "I don't really know. Well, that's not strictly true. I wanted to apologize for leaving the other day." He looks away as if embarrassed.

"That's okay," I reply gently.

"No, it's more than that. I need to apologize for my behavior… in the past."

I suck in a breath at his words. He must hear me because his eyebrows pull inward, concern crossing his model-like features. "I'm not entirely sure I remember every way that I behaved badly, I just know I did. *A lot.* It was unfair and uncalled for. I know you were trying to help me back then. I should never have taken out my pain on you." He looks at me and once again I'm trapped. "I'm sorry," he whispers, although I'm not quite sure he's saying it to me.

"You said that already," I whisper back. His eyes leave mine and he looks down to his cup. "Ruben, is that the only reason you came back?" I ask. Even as the words leave my mouth, I'm not sure that I want to know the answer. *Hell, I don't know why I even asked it.* His truths could be my truths. Since he left last time, I've built my walls up higher, learned how to shut everything and nearly everyone off. I don't want to live like this, afraid of everything. I just don't know any other way to be. Everything seems to slow down as Ruben's muscle jumps in his jaw. He seems to be having some kind of internal struggle.

"I'm not sure exactly. I just needed to see you, Laurie," he answers.

I feel off balance as my world stops, breaks open, and for the first time in what feels like forever… a light shines through.

Ruben

I'm not sure why I just said that. If the look on Laurie's face is anything to go by, then I just said too damn much. *Fuck.*

"I'm sorry," I tell her. *All I seem to do is apologize to this woman.*

"N-no, it's fine. I just…" she huffs out a sigh, "…Ruben, I don't understand?"

That make's two of us, sweetheart.

"I have no real explanation. I don't understand myself. I came here… I'm not really sure why to be honest. I thought it was to ask you for your help, I mean, I'm not good with those classes you run. So, I was going to ask for some one-on-one time with you, but whenever I look at you…" I stop speaking, not wanting to continue that thought process.

"Whenever you look at me, what?" she pushes.

I stare into her eyes, captured once again, by the mixture of pain and tenderness, almost at odds with each other. "When I look at you, I feel like *you're* the one that needs help. You look… caught. I'm not sure how. I'm not even sure how to explain it, but when I look at you, I see your demons. I've never been able to see past my own before."

"What exactly do you want to do? Fix me?" Her angry whisper hides a deeper emotion that I can't quite put my finger on.

I rub my head. "I don't know, Laurie, okay?" I try not to snap.

"No. It's not okay!" she snaps back, louder, and the few people in the diner look up. Before I say anything she continues, "You were horrible to me eighteen months ago. Maybe I should let that lie, but Ruben, *it hurt*. I tried to help you and you dismissed me like a cold caller."

"I was in pain," I growl out.

"Aren't we all?" she hisses back.

I slouch down in my seat and sigh. "Maybe coming here wasn't the right thing to do," I tell her.

"Maybe it wasn't," Laurie replies sharply. She takes a sip of her coffee and blows out a breath.

"Look, you're here now, do you still want to do one-on-one?" she offers.

I pull a hand down my face. "Okay, the truth…" I mumble to myself, "…Laurie, I'd like some one-on-one, but honestly, I feel like I'm getting better like I'm nearly there. I mean, sure, I have some issues that still need dealing with, things that Anabel has been helping me work through."

"Then why do you want one-on-one time with me?" she asks, confusion clear in her eyes.

"Because I think you still have demons. Ones that aren't going anywhere soon. One's that you're not facing right now. Laurie, I want to help you… I thought we could help each other," I tell her and wait. Then wait some more. She doesn't say anything, just sits staring at me. Her eyes work, but I don't know her well enough to *always* see what's going on behind the façade.

"Thanks, but no thanks," she tells me, getting up from her seat. "Thanks for the coffee." Her voice has gone back to the angelic natural tone and I nod in response. Of everything I've learned over the last twelve months, the main lesson is that you can't force people to see their demons, and you can't force them to deal with their issues. You can't help someone who doesn't want to help themselves. Laurie once told me that.

What's Left of Me

She starts to walk away, but I grab her arm. "I'll walk with you," I tell her. She snatches her arm away, but sighs and nods, which I take as an agreement.

As we leave the diner, we fall into an awkward silence. "Do you spend all your time at the community center?" I ask, moving onto safer conversational grounds.

"Not all my time, but yeah, a big chunk of it. I came here about a year after… Anyway, at first, the center was my home because the people here helped me. Then, Derick—"

"Derick?" I ask

"He's the manager. Such a lovely guy, about sixty, he's been running the place for forever. Of course, he wants to retire soon. The only problem then will be funding, and obviously the lack of a manager. Anyway, I'm getting off track. So Derick offered me a cleaning job. I was desperate for the money, I'd do anything, plus keeping busy was a bonus especially back then. I spent all my free time at the community center. I had nothing but time." She swallows and looks down at her feet. "I had no home back then, and I don't mean metaphorically, I mean in the literal sense. Derick let me use one of the sofas in the communal room, every night after the center was shut, so I had somewhere safe and warm to sleep. I started doing some of the paperwork, mainly helping out because I was bored. Quickly, I learned the ropes but didn't get paid. It passed the time, plus I figured, it gave me skills for the real world.

The woman who did all the office work back then, Edna, was Derick's wife. She retired about eight months after I started coming here, so he offered me the job. Apart from Rocco's birth, it was the single biggest thing that had ever happened to me in my life." She stops and looks up at me. "That's pretty sad, right? I mean the biggest things to ever happen to me were my nephew being born and being offered an office manager job?" Her lips twitch. "Funny, I don't feel sad about those things, I only feel proud and blessed." She starts walking again, but I'm stuck. This beautiful woman–Fuck, did I just refer to her as beautiful?–has so much more strength than she realizes. She has a huge heart and does everything with a smile.

Laurie stops. "You okay?" she questions and it jolts me from my daze.

"Yeah." My voice is raspy as I join her, stepping into her side.

She starts walking slowly, glancing up at me. "You really want to know this stuff?" she asks, insecurity in her tone.

"Yeah, strangely enough, I do. I find you interesting, and I'm actually pretty bummed that nearly two years ago when you started trying to help me, I pushed you away. I couldn't see the genuine care you had or the fact that you wanted nothing but to actually help me and I threw that in your face." My stomach twists with a stabbing pain when I think about how I pushed her away. Even back then I thought she was beautiful, but I couldn't admit it, not even to myself. I was too hung up on Amanda, and I thought if I even looked at another woman I'd be betraying her.

Laurie blushes as we come to a stop outside the center. I step toward her. "You make me look at everything differently," I tell her.

"W-what do you mean?" she asks as I move that little bit closer. Bringing my hand up without really thinking about what I'm doing, my fingers find a strand of her hair and I tuck it behind her ear. Little intimate touches like these I've tried to avoid with anyone for so long, but there's always been a draw to this woman for me, something I controlled by cutting her out of my life.

"The world seems different when I'm with you…" I explain, letting my fingers stroke slowly down her cheek, "…being around you." I sigh. "Laurie, you make the impossible seem like a walk in the park. With you, I feel like I'm capable of anything. You make me want everything, all the things I'd thought were never possible again.

Everything... it's all wrapped up in you. I'm only just seeing it now. Seeing *you* now."

"Ruben, I'm not sure what you're saying," she whispers. When she stares at me, her eyes push through every external wall of bullshit I've built up throughout my whole life. She doesn't just *slay* my demons, she *decimates* them, just with her smile or her voice. Just by standing next to me.

I can't say the feelings don't scare me. But now I'm stronger than I've ever been, with Danny and Anabel helping me exorcise the demons I was still clinging to, from Amanda's passing.

"I'd like to help out at the center if that's okay?"

She's taken aback by my offer. "Okay. I mean, sure, thanks. We can always use volunteers. Is there anything you're particularly good at?" she asks me.

I take a few moments to think. "Well, I can spend time with the old folks? If you have something there?"

"Yeah, that would be great. Just sitting and talking to them, giving them time would be great. It's not an area that most people want to volunteer in."

"Well, my mom had me when she was forty-one, she's seventy-eight now and she has Alzheimer's. So I kind of have some experience. She lives with my aunt, has done for a few years, but I visit regularly. It's been hard watching her demise, seeing her turn into someone she's not, forgetting everything. She would hate it if she realized what was happening. I hate it for her."

Laurie nods and I'm surprised by my own admission. There's something about this woman that makes me want to be honest… about everything. Like there's a need within me, a need to lay myself bare. *For her.*

"Okay. Well, tomorrow the old folks come to the center, and they're here all day. So come whenever, okay?" she asks me. Her eyes find mine again, the easy going smile on her face hits me in the gut and I take a step back. "Ruben, are you sure you're okay?" she asks again.

I nod then reply, "Tomorrow, Laurie," before turning on my heel and heading back home, only this time it doesn't feel like I'm running. I need a check in with Anabel. I'm hoping that at some point soon my emotions will settle, instead of being so up and down. It's as though all my feelings are being thrown in the air and I'm being told to catch them. I'm looking forward to a time when I don't need to speak to Anabel to pull apart my thoughts and emotions. Needing to be sure that the road I'm crawling along is my path, and all the effort is worth it, so eventually I won't be crawling I'll be running.

Chapter Seven

Laurie

I walk back into the community center slightly dazed. Luckily or unluckily—as the case may be right about now—Sarah is on hand to snap me out of it, seemingly waiting for my return.

"Tell me everything!" she demands, gripping onto my forearm when I'm no more than two steps in through the door. I roll my eyes, but follow her lead to the coffee room as she tugs on my arm, pushing the scratchy knit material into my skin. It's better to get this done. I still have cleaning to finish. Pushing us both down on the soft chairs, that sit out of place in the coffee room.

This area is bare, necessities are the only things gracing the counter tops. The two chairs we sit in were donated. We had a young woman come here—she was isolated after being attacked—and with Sarah's help, she got better learning to live in the real world. Her parents were grateful and they were also rich. That year we didn't have to find the fifty thousand dollars that we barely scrape together every year, just to keep this place running. We also found ourselves with a few new items. These two chairs being some of the goods that were given.

Placing my arms along the edges of the seat, I scrunch the soft, luxurious brown material in between my fingers. It's a silly comfort I know well. Even when I lived at home with my parents, we never had anything as grand as these. I've been known, on occasion, to come and sit in one of these chairs after my day is done. Needing some peace and quiet, and very aware that when Amber's not there, the house I live in is not even close to being a real home. The lack of anything warm or inviting in the small space doesn't help in filling me with the comfort and homeliness that I crave so desperately.

"It was… strange."

"Strange? What kind of an answer is that?" Sarah replies, looking slightly deflated. She juts her bottom lip out and blows up, fanning her bangs away from her face. At nearly forty-three, Sarah has it going on. With her tiny, almost pixie-like frame, and platinum blonde hair to match, she just needs wings to be an extra in a *Tinkerbell* movie. The years have been good to her skin. Always using moisturizer, she says. But I've seen her mom, I know she just lucked out and has good genes.

I pull my lips to one side of my face and scrunch up my nose. "I don't know what exactly happened. It was… strange," I murmur.

"There's that word again." She blows up at her bangs once more and I stand up, reaching into my pocket and pulling out two spare bobby pins. "Thanks." She winks at me and puts one pin in her front teeth while using the other to pull some of the overly long hair—that's about a month overdue a cut, and the reason why it's getting into her eyes—between her fingers and clips it out of the way. "So start from the beginning. What happened?" she asks through her teeth, the second pin still sticking out. And even though she looks like *Tinkerbell* right now, she reminds me of the wild animals on those shows, picking the carcasses of their prey from between their teeth.

"He took me for a coffee. He said his first thought for coming here was to ask for help, in the form of one-on-one sessions with me."

Sarah raises her eyebrows and makes a groaning sound.

"Woman! You're supposed to be a dang counselor!" My exasperated voice is only bettered slightly by my hands, which I throw into the air in an *'I don't believe you'* pose.

Sarah laughs, slapping her hands on her thighs. "Girl, I'm not in counselor mode right now. I'm fully immersed in girlfriend mode. If I couldn't differentiate between my work and my personal life, I'd have no friends," she tells me throwing her arm out with flare and jingling the different colored bangles she always wears up her arm.

"Okay," I giggle. "Calm down." The humor infused into my tone is something Sarah always manages to bring out in me, it's one of the reasons we've been friends since I met her. I never laughed much, not after Rocco and Larissa. "Anyway, while he was talking about me helping him, something changed. I have no idea what, I could just see his features... they morphed, they became soft. He looked at me like—"

"Like?" she demands.

"Like he could see me. Like he saw into my soul." I shake my head. "God, I sound ridiculous," I chastise myself.

"Stop. Don't do that, don't belittle what you felt. It doesn't matter whether it was there or not, it only matters that *you* felt it. It was tangible to *you* Laurie, so it *did* exist, it *did* happen," she says softly, moving her head down to catch my eyes, which I'd direct to the floor.

"Separating your work and personal life, huh?" I ask smugly.

Sarah rolls her eyes. "Well, if you're going to talk stupid, then I need to bring out my other side," she tells me and I giggle again.

My giggles stop abruptly when I think back to his words. "He said I have demons that I need to work through, things I'm hiding from." I glance to her face, expecting to see shock, or maybe a frown. Instead, her eyes are cast downward and her mouth is pinched. "Sarah?" Her name is a question on my lips as an unease spreads through me.

"I'm sorry girl, I hate to say this, but that man can see through the front you have in place."

"What?" the whisper drops from my lips as my eyes widen.

"I agree with him. You have issues, I believe that to be true. But baby girl, you are *not* ready to face them."

I stand up so quickly, I'm almost shocked. "I do *not* have issues," I hiss out between my clenched teeth.

"Yep. That's what I figured your response would be. Sit down Laurie, tell me what else he said," she coaxes me. Her face is a cover, soft and placid, I've seen her use this face when she's needed to help the most vulnerable or scared of our visitors. Kids who don't want to talk, but desperately need help. *Is that how she sees me?* I sit back down, feeling uneasy, I'm just not sure why.

"He changed the subject. Asked if he could help out here," I explain her, watching her face closely. Sarah nods at me. "Stop it," I snap.

"Stop what?" her tone is level, all the character that I usually hear in her voice has gone.

"Stop being a shrink. I hate it," I complain looking at the floor once again.

"Hey girl, I'm sorry, it's hard to pull myself away from it sometimes. After all, this is also part of me," she tells me and I feel bad for snapping at her.

I cross my arms over my body and rub the tops of my arms up and down. Sarah's eyes follow my hands, watching my movements. Suddenly feeling self-conscious, I stop and bring my hands back to my lap.

"Anyway, he's coming tomorrow, he's going to sit with the old folks," I explain.

Her eyes light up at that statement. "Oh wow! That will be great. They have hardly any interaction," she says jubilantly.

I just nod. It's true, no one really cares about the old folks. They live in a home about two miles away, and come here three times a week, just to get away from there. We lay on as much as we can for them, but in truth, it's probably not any better than being at the home. Having someone new to talk to will hopefully bring them out of their shells.

"I better get back to the cleaning," I say, standing.

Sarah stands with me, catching my arm before I walk away. "Listen, Laurie. You don't want to hear this, and I get it, you're not ready. But just know that I'm here if you need me. We all have things that we hide from one another. Sometimes small things, sometimes huge. What most of us forget… choosing instead to hide them, even from ourselves… is that these things… they all make you who you are. Without them, you'd be a different version of yourself. Not better, not worse, just different. That's okay too, being different. Sometimes we need to move into different, just to move forward. The main thing is that you're not scared. That you surround yourself with people who love you. One person or one hundred… it doesn't matter. Just knowing that someone's there who loves you, and will catch you should you fall. That person can help you become who you want. That person can give you freedom from your own chains." Her eyes search mine, pleading with me to hear her, and I do, I just don't want to admit it out loud. So I pull my arm from her grip and walk away. Ignoring the pain that has started to bubble up from the pit of my stomach, ever since Ruben Asher came back into my damn life and brought back all my truths.

Chapter EIGHT

Ruben

"Uncle Wuben, can we puway wiff da hamsterwer." Mandie's words are mumbled. At four, I'm not sure whether this is how she should speak or not. I look to Anabel, who rolls her eyes at me.

"She asked if you could both play with Lucky, the hamster," she explains pointing to the little brown and white furry ball, which sits trembling in the corner of a wired cage. My eyes move from the terrified creature to Anabel and Danny's oldest child, Amanda—lovingly nicknamed Mandie. Then my eyes graze across the thick, cream, shag-pile carpet until they reach Clara, their nearly two-year-old terror. Currently proving my point, with a carrot stick, that she seems to be trying to shove up the ass of a toy duck. Can't say the duck looks impressed, plastic or not.

I move my gaze back to Mandie. "Sure, baby doll, you wanna get him out for me?" I ask.

"Nah-uh, Mama says it has to be a groaned up." Her little girl hands are on her hips, and with the sass she has, even at four, she reminds me of Anabel, who promptly chuckles at her daughter.

"Okay." I sigh and reach in to get the fuzzy mass. I pull him up and into my hand, holding him gently while he continues to tremble away. Mandie reaches over slowly and softly strokes his fur the correct way, telling me that's how she's been shown, and that I should do the same. After a few minutes I start to loosen up, Mandie is obviously a pro at looking after the little rodent nestled in my palm. He seems to have stopped shivering, which I'm taking as a good sign. Then without warning Clara picks up a xylophone throwing it from her chubby little fingers straight across the room. Now *that* child is one hundred percent her daddy. The noise startles Lucky, who simultaneously craps in my hand while biting my finger.

"Ahh, shit!" I shout, tipping my hand up the other way, but instead of the little beast dropping to the floor, he hangs from my hand, his teeth piercing my finger as he holds on for dear life.

"Mind your mouth!" Anabel shouts.

What's Left of Me

"Fuck that shit! This little fucker won't let go! Fuck!" I yell, waving my hand around, trying to dislodge the damn animal. Nothing seems to be working. Anabel gives me a dirty look as she steps over to where I've ended up, taking over, trying to pry the little bastard from my hand. Things don't get any easier when Mandie says *'Fuck that shit,'* followed by Clara getting up, her podgy little legs pushing her forward as she tries to run to the now broken xylophone, saying *'Fuck'* repeatedly, over and over and over again, the whole way across the room.

Once Anabel has removed the cling-on, she slaps me upside the head. "Go get your hand cleaned up dickwad, this isn't over," she hisses quietly to me.

Four hours later and Anabel has forgiven me... just. Danny just raises his eyebrows as she retells the story to him. We're sitting once again in their back yard, I'm freezing my balls off but also following the lead of my friends.

"So what did you come here for today?" Anabel asks. It's a fair question. I've been here for half the day and haven't said why. Let's face it, the house has been too chaotic.

I sit back and take a swig of my water. "I went back to see Laurie."

"What! Why? What's going on?" Danny interrupts.

"Danny shhh! I filled you in yesterday remember?" Anabel grumbles waving her hand at him to shut up while still looking at me.

I chuckle to myself as Danny gives me the finger. "I saw that," Anabel snaps and Danny's lips twitch. "Go on," she urges me.

"Nothing really." I shrug.

"Nothing?" Her face moves into a frown and she leans forward slightly. "Elaborate, Ruben," she demands and I smirk for a second before I think about Laurie's reaction to what I'd said yesterday and my smile drops.

"I told her, I think that she has demons. One's she hasn't faced yet."

"Oh, I bet she just loved you," Anabel says shaking her head laughing.

"What? What did I do?" I ask.

"Oh, Ruben. You haven't seen her for eighteen months and you didn't exactly end things well. Now you waltz back into her life, actually no, into one of her sessions. You've probably thrown her completely by being there, and then you run out, only to go back and tell her you think *she* has issues." Anabel stares at me.

"Shit," I groan, allowing my head to flop backward, realizing what an absolute dick I've been.

"Ruben there's something else I want to say." I look back to her. "Listen, you can always come to Danny or me, we'll always be here for you. Especially if you want to talk about Amanda. But as far as I can see you're there now."

"There?" I question.

"Yeah. *There.* You're ready to move on. Find someone else. You're pretty much healed, and anything else past this point can't come from us. It can only come from you, and from whoever you give your heart to. Trust in them and trust in you."

I sigh, but nod. I know she's right. I think about Amanda and she'll always have a place in my heart, a part of me will always love her, but I'm ready to move on now. I never thought I would be, but here I am. Now, I just need to allow myself that freedom.

The next morning I find myself standing outside of the community center. I'm hopping from foot to foot awkwardly, partly because it's freaking cold and partly because I'm unsure what to do next. The lack of self-confidence is something I'm not used to, always having bravado, especially with women—that was *before Amanda*. After I had lost her, alcohol was my crutch. For the four years that I relied on it, I didn't need confidence, because I didn't care about anything or anyone, even myself. The final part of my journey, before coming back here, has been to get clean and to try and work all my issues out. The confidence I once had hasn't been needed for so long, I'm worried I don't know how to really interact with unfamiliar people nowadays.

I haven't done anything substantial in my company for so long. Danny hired a guy—David—and he's been running things. I get weekly updates, as did Danny until recently, now I'm trying to take a more active role again. I've also not been with a woman since Amanda. I've not even thought about it, until now. Too stuck in the past, or wallowing in my own self-pity.

Kicking a stone, I glance around. *Come on Ruben, suck it up.*

"Hey. You're Ruben, right?" I hear from the side of me. So consumed with my own thoughts, I didn't see the little pixie-like woman, the same woman that got Laurie for me when I came here yesterday.

"Oh, yeah, hey," I say with a half-smile.

What's Left of Me

"You don't have to look so nervous, sugar. I don't bite... mostly," she tells me with a smirk.

She's joking... I think.

"I'm Sarah, come on, I'll show you around," she says, tucking her small arm through mine, a rattling coming from all the jewelry she has running up her wrist.

I take in the center as Sarah drifts from room to room with me alongside her. The passion she has for the place is evident in everything she does.

"This is where the elderly folk are," she tells me, as we step into the only room she hasn't yet introduced me to. Immediately, I notice that no one moves as we enter. Not a single one of the ten seniors looks up in acknowledgment, or even curiosity, wondering who's just entered the room.

"What's wrong with them?" my whisper brings Sarah's gaze to mine.

"Come," she suggests, stepping back through the door. "Let's go to the coffee room." I nod and follow.

Pointing me to a chair when we walk into the bare room, she moves to the coffee pot. "You have to understand..." Sarah begins her back to me while making our coffees. As I listen to her, I look around, taking in the depressing room. A room that's supposed to be an escape from daily work. "The old folks come here to get away from Meadow Senior Living, but they don't really have anything different here than there." She turns and brings our coffees to us, taking the seat next to me.

"Why?" I ask simply.

Sarah shrugs her shoulders. "Funding mainly. But it's more than that. We don't have enough people to volunteer. Me, Laurie, and Derick are the only ones who get paid. We've had people come and go over the years, doing stints of volunteering, but nobody ever sticks around for long. Makes things harder… you know?"

I don't really know, so I say nothing in response.

"Is Laurie here?" my words are almost whispered.

"Damn, sugar, you got it bad," Sarah comments smacking me across the knee. "She'll be here soon, probably doing something with Amber."

"Amber?" I ask.

"Nuh-uh, her life, her stories, if she wants to share, that's on her."

I nod and grin. Many a woman I've known would gladly spill her friend's shit. Good to know that some women can keep that stuff tight, and more, Laurie has that in Sarah.

"Right sugar, as much fun as it is spending time with you, I have work to do. A counselor always has work to do," she tells me with a wink. "I'll take you down to the seniors, introduce you, then just be yourself. Chat or watch television with them, whatever you feel comfortable with. When Laurie comes in, I'll point her in your direction and she can have a chat with you about your plans here." I nod again and follow her down the dingy hall, wondering how different it would be if this place were somewhere that brightened the spirits of people who desperately needed it. All the while knowing, it's not just the visitors that need their days brightening and it's not just the visitors days that I want to brighten.

Chapter Nine

Laurie

"I'm so tired this morning, why are you dragging me here again?" Amber moans as she sits next to me on the bus. When I smile in response, she rolls her eyes and puts her earphones in, I can just hear the tinny noise pumping out, probably scarring her eardrums. Amber turns into a typical teen if you wake her before eight am. Today, I want her help at the community center. She never complains, the place was home for her until she moved in with me, plus helping out there added to her gaining the scholarship.

I made the mistake of telling her about Ruben's visit. Her initial feelings were of anger. They were spat out through her mouthful of chili… it was absolutely delightful. When I explained that he had offered to help out with the seniors, her feelings toward him softened some. Then she threw me completely, when, after telling her how Ruben said he thought I still had issues to work through, Amber told me flat out the she agreed with him. Before she went to bed last night, while I was making lunch for today, I told her that I needed her help at the center. She shook her head smirking, then walked over and sat down next to me, patted my hand like I was a scared child and said, *'I'll protect you'* then she winked, giggled to herself, and walked off to bed. My mouth hung open, and I stammered trying to say something, anything. Nothing came out. This morning, her reaction wasn't quite as helpful as she pulled the covers over her head, and told me to deal with Ruben on my own. That I was a big girl and she needed to sleep. I managed to drag her up, but she's been grumpy ever since.

"Morning, your man's here," Sarah tells me the minute I walk into the center. She has an unmistakable twinkle in her eye.

Amber huffs out and follows through with yet another eye roll. "I'm going to dump my stuff and then head to the games room," she grumbles.

"Morning Sarah, good to see you," Sarah says to Amber with heavy sarcasm.

I watch as Amber's shoulders drop and she turns around, a sheepish look on her face. "Sorry Sarah, morning," she replies with a small, embarrassed grin that makes one of her dimples pop out. The she rushes off, and I look back at Sarah, who bursts into laughter.

"You're gonna miss that one when she goes." The smile on her face vanishes as she takes in my reaction to her words. "Sorry baby. I forget that when she goes, it's not gonna be easy on you."

I bite my bottom lip and hold my hand up to her, indicating I need a second to compose myself. "It doesn't matter…" I croak out, "…she's going to be amazing, and this will be the start of the life she's always deserved. I'm over the moon for her." My words linger like wasps in the air, and I'm waiting for the sting to come.

"I know what you're saying is true, but I also know you, honey. I can see in your eyes the struggle that you're constantly fighting when it comes to Amber leaving. You've built your life around her for the last two years, I'm not sure you're ready for her to go. Telling yourself that you are, and actually feeling that way, are two different things." Sarah's words are kind, they're meant to be a comfort blanket, soothing away my ailments, but all they do is serve to bring everything I'm trying to avoid thinking about up to the surface.

What's Left of Me

"Where's Ruben?" My change in both topic and tone causes a reaction in Sarah. It's only a small head movement, and probably unnoticeable to most, but I catch it. Sarah is the master of disguise. Being a counselor she needs to hide her emotions, and when the topic is serious, she's been known to mask reactions extremely well. The fact that I just caused a recoil from her, however small, tells me what I already don't want to know. My avoidance issues have hit an all-time high, even I know that the end is near. I need to face what's coming and get ready to sort all the crap out in my head. Because if I don't, the demons I live with aren't going to just surface, they're going to take over, and I'm not sure there'll be anything of me left behind when they do.

"He's in the rec room with the seniors."

I blink twice and look at Sarah, trying to remember what question I'd asked her. When my thoughts catch up, I nod. As I walk away, she grabs my arm and I turn back to her.

A look of unmistakable concern covers her face and she offers me a small smile. "I'm here. When you're ready, I'll be here." I pull in my eyebrows, but nod once again before turning, needing to find Ruben.

"So what happened then?" Ruben's excited voice carries down the corridor, hitting me in the chest, making my body sway. As I approach the door, I slow and come to a stop. Leaning against the doorframe, without even really understanding what I'm doing, I watch Ruben and Mr. Pallor.

"Well, we ran," Mr. Pallor replies with a chuckle. The usually quiet, elderly, somewhat frail man, is now animated. His eyes sparkle and his arms have taken on a life of their own. The thin, almost see through skin, covering the back of his hands, the blood spots dotted across his wrists and the sunken, nearly skeletal look of his face have all been forgotten. Disappeared amongst the stories of yesteryear. I feel my heart warm, but decide to leave them be. The seniors need someone new to listen to them.

As I walk away, I think about how Mr. Pallor is different to the others. Dementia has taken a hold of him, stripping his memories, his independence, and sometimes his dignity. It's a truly vile disease, and I can't imagine how he feels when the moments of clarity break through. It's the people connected to him, who have to watch the suffering that I sometimes feel sorrier for. Having to live through your loved one being ripped from your life... from *their own* life, must be heart-breaking.

The times he's been clear minded, he's managed to talk to me. He's told me his truths, explained how trapped he is inside his own shell, his prison. That he's a stranger to himself and feeling scared is an almost constant for him. The majority of his time these days is spent not recognizing anyone, anything, or anywhere. He said, sometimes he wishes, those moments he sinks back into the real world, would stop happening. That they can be more painful than anything. It's in those moments, his brain clicks onto the fact that everything else was a lie. He said what's worse, is that he knows he's heading right back underwater, and there's nothing he can do to stop it.

"Hey Laurie, can you help me with something?" Marco, one of the boys who frequents the center asks, pulling me from my sad thoughts as I climb the stairs.

"Yeah, sure. What do you need?" I ask looking up at the top of the stairs, into his worried brown eyes, as I take my last few steps.

"You know I've been trying to do my GED? Well, I'm struggling and I can't fuck this up, Laurie," he says passing his work to me, which I start looking at.

"Language," I chastise with a sideways glance.

"Sorry, ma'am," Marco answers.

Shit, how old am I? When did I become a ma'am?

"Okay, listen. I could help you, but honestly, between work here and the fact that I'm just not that good, I'm probably not your best bet." I chuckle. "It's been many years since I've been to school. And let me tell you, I scraped by the first time, only with the help of my sister." My mirth dies down as I think about Larissa. A pang rumbles in my stomach—it's the realization that I don't remember her every day anymore. I shake my head, hoping to push out the thoughts. "Listen, Amber is somewhere here. Go look for her. You know she'll help," I tell him and watch as his eyes sparkle. All the boys that come here have a thing for Amber. At once he nods, mumbles his thanks and spins around walking off to find her.

"Ah-hmm," I semi cough out, trying to mask my laughter.

Looking over his shoulder, Marco's tanned cheeks redden slightly as he shuffles back, relieving me of his paperwork, before rushing away again.

Two hours later, and the mountain of paperwork I found in the small admin office is now more of a hill. Sighing and rubbing my temples, my immediate thoughts are of coffee. After filling my cup, I remember Ruben. I'm not sure if he's still here, but I decide to go find out. Putting my cup down and automatically walking back to where he was earlier, I see he's moved positions, now sitting on the old man's other side. The other five seniors are all sitting facing Mr. Pallor too. Although, I think they're more interested in Ruben.

"Then they appeared from the back of the holding cells and we didn't know what to do," the old man tells Ruben, who could easily be his grandson.

"So what happened then?" Ruben asks eagerly.

"Well, we ran," Mr. Pallor replies with a chuckle. That moment it dawns on me that Ruben is listening to the same story again. Maybe for the hundredth time, still holding the same interest and excitement on his face that he did when I saw it being relayed to him earlier. I step back from the door, my heartbeat causing a whooshing in my ears. The compassion that he so obviously feels winds me, and I need a moment. Sliding down the wall and bringing my knees up to my chest, I'm glad the hallway is empty. I take deep breaths trying desperately not to think about Ruben, but he's taken over my mind.

"Dammit," I whisper to myself.

The more time I spend with this man, the more I realize it's like he's been created just for me. Every part of him specifically picked to suit my needs and wants. That also means, though, knowing how much he's been through, and that he could never love someone again—those words coming from his own mouth—that I'm setting myself up for one monumental fall. And if I lose someone else I love… I'm not sure I'd recover. *Not again.*

Chapter Ten

Ruben

Ronnie tells me his story again. I assume the name he's given me is correct, but I also know Dementia causes a lot of truths to be forgotten. The story of Ronnie's time in World War Two, can't be the only one he has, but it's the only one he's sharing. I've listened to him tell me it seven times in the last two hours. It's only in the past thirty minutes that the other seniors have started to take an interest in what's going on. I assume they've heard the repeated story and, therefore, switch off. I've spoken briefly to Mildred, who wouldn't give me her full name, insisting I call her Mildred so as not to make her feel old. The other four seniors, all women, are very quiet. They seemed bored when I came in, now they seem to be watchful, inquisitive. Not enough to partake in the conversation, though.

"I'm going to get a coffee Ronnie, you want one?" I ask the man who was just alight with pleasure. Now he sits there staring out of the window, like an empty vessel. It chokes me up. My mom is like this now too. *I should see her more often.* Shaking my head and offer coffee to everyone else, who all decline, so I move out of the room almost falling over a body crouched on the floor.

"Laurie?" I ask, surprised.

She looks up to me, her eyes are wide, some of her dark hair is stuck to her face. She looks like a rabbit caught in the headlights, and if it's possible, it makes her even more appealing.

"Ruben." The soft tone of her voice flows out as a whisper. I hold my arm out to her and she slips her small hand into mine. Pulling her up to me, there's less than an inch between us. I recognize right then that I want to kiss this woman, and maybe never stop. Our eyes are helping us engage in a standoff as we gaze at one another. When I can take no more, my feet maneuver me a step back, giving us both space. Laurie blinks and seems to gather her thoughts.

"I was… coffee, do you want a coffee?" she rushes the words out.

I rub the back of my neck and try to suppress a smile, everything about this woman causes a reaction in me. "Yeah, that's where I was heading, too."

Nodding, Laurie spins around and makes her way to the break room that Sarah took me to earlier. She walks silently, and I can just imagine the thoughts that are going through her head, trying to organize them and construct them in such a way, so that she can keep me at arm's length.

"So, who's Amber?" I ask.

Her step falters, but she quickly corrects it. "Who told you about Amber?" she replies not turning around to face me.

"Sarah, but she wouldn't say anymore. Said it was your story to tell," I reply.

Laurie doesn't say anything more, and I think that's it. That she's not going to share. However, once we have our coffees and have taken a seat, Laurie rests her elbows on her knees and leans forward. Her shoulders drop and she lets out a sigh. "She was a runaway. Kept being placed in children's homes and continuously leaving. We found her in the doorway one day, half-starved and freezing. Once we got her sorted out, the system wanted to suck her right back in. I kept her with me for longer than I was allowed. The authorities found out, and that's when Sarah stepped in. She has friends over in adoptive services. Between them, they managed to swing it so she could stay in my care, with extremely close monitoring." She looks up to my face now as she bites her lip. "She's been a crutch for me, and I'm only just working that out now. The other thing I've worked out very recently is that apparently everyone can see just how damaged I am. I've been trying to kid myself for so long…" Laurie stops talking and drops her head again. I'm at a loss, unsure what I'm supposed to do. This is what I wanted, for her to admit that she has issues, to face them, to overcome them. I still don't know why it's so important to me? Why I want to help so badly? Why I can even *see* her issues? Now she has admitted it, though, I'm stuck. I don't know which direction to take.

"Doesn't matter," I hear her whisper, and it sends a bolt of anger through me. Annoyed with myself for not doing the one thing I have been asking… to be there for her.

"Fuck it!" I slam my hand down on the table and Laurie's head jerks up.

"What?" Her eyebrows shoot skyward, worry mixed with confusion covers her face.

"I'm taking you out tonight," I tell her.

"W-what?" she stammers.

"Simple. I've known you for over two years, Laurie, but I don't really *know* you. Tonight, that changes. And it's not just me that's going to learn all about you, Laurie. Tonight I want *you,* to get to know *the real you.* I have a feeling that you don't really have the first clue about yourself, about who you really are, or what you really want. I'd bet that you've lived for everyone else almost your whole life. I'm gonna help you make that change, and I'm gonna help you live for *you*."

When I see the tears that well in her eyes, I know I've hit a nerve. She ignores the lone tear that rolls down her cheek, instead biting her lip as the corners of her mouth tip up in a small smile. Then she nods. It's the only response I get before I watch her silently walk out of the room.

"You ready?" My voice startles Laurie, who seems to be in her own head as she stares out of the office window a few hours later.

"Huh?" she replies, tilting her head.

"It's after four, I'm taking you for dinner," I tell her.

"Oh, yeah, right," she mumbles back. "Wait, no. I don't normally leave here until after six and I eat even later than that. There's so much to do still, I can't leave yet."

What's Left of Me

"No arguing. You deserve an early finish. I've already told Sarah that I'm taking you for dinner, and she's gonna drop Amber back home."

"What? You don't even know Sarah, and yet you're organizing my life through her?" The growl that comes out of her mouth surprises me. When we interacted all that time ago, even though for a lot of it I was drunk, or angry and therefore ignored her, she never—that I remember—got angry that much. Quickly pushing past her mood, I smile.

Her scowl drops, as she lets her eyes move over my face. "You're so h—" She stops mid-sentence, but I let it slide.

"Come on, you need to eat," I say pointing to her tiny frame. With no reply, she stands and grabs her purse. I lead her out of the center and to my car, opening the door for her to get in. All the while, not a word is spoken.

It's not until we're ten minutes along in our journey that the silence is broken. "Where are we going?" Her voice is quiet, almost timid, even though I know that she's not.

"To my apartment."

"What?"

My reply obviously shocks her, if her replied screech is anything to go by. "I figured you know I'm not an axe murderer. I thought it would be nice going somewhere quiet, peaceful, a place where we could talk or just kick back." My answer is only part truth. I did want to go somewhere quiet so we could talk. However, the real reason I picked my place is because I know that Laurie doesn't have much money. She may not have something suitable to wear at such short notice for a nice restaurant, and I know she'd try and pay for her half… even though there's no way in hell I'd let her. I don't want to put her in an awkward position, and I don't give one shit what she wears or where we are. As long as I can spend time with this woman, I will. I want to know everything, and tonight that mission officially starts.

Chapter Eleven

Laurie

I'm still not entirely sure how I ended up at Ruben's apartment. There was a time, when I first met him, I thought that I could help him. Back then, I would have given anything to be alone at his place. With nothing more than a few dates and the odd kiss here and there, my love life hasn't really consisted of much *love*… then again the *life* part sucks most of the time too. Now I'm here, I'm reminded about the valley that seems to sit between us. The whole situation feels strange, and yet comfortable. I can't read anything into that, though. Although I've known Ruben for years, I really know nothing about him, and I'm sure he feels the same about me.

We enter his place, which is less like an apartment and more like one of those designer pads. The ones they have on those television shows, where someone has to sell them for the owner and they nearly always reach at least a million dollars. I realize that I need to use the bathroom, I'm not sure whether it's because of a genuine need, or because I'm so nervous that I'm about to pee myself.

"Can you tell me where the bathroom is?" I ask Ruben. I'm pretty sure he can sense my worry, if his scrunched up eyebrows are any indication.

He doesn't call me on it, though, only pointing in the direction I assume is the location of the bathroom. I nod and make my way along the hallway. For such a big place, there doesn't seem to be too many doors, so I find the bathroom immediately. What I see when I enter takes my breath away. The room is nicer than my bedroom and living space all rolled into one. Hell, it's nicer than *all* the bedrooms and living spaces I've ever lived in throughout my whole life, rolled into one. The room is huge and filled with dark gray marble, some white tiling obviously used to lighten the place up. Double basins and double shower and fluffy gray and white towels. It screams man… no… it screams bachelor. But all very sterile and not a home. It's only after I do my business and reach over to grab some toilet paper that I really appreciate the luxury. The tissue is soft on my fingers, I could probably use it for my face or to stuff my currently hollow pillow.

"His toilet paper probably costs more than the clothes I'm wearing," I mumble the words to myself and they sound so ridiculous that I start laughing, on the toilet, with Ruben in the next room. Stifling my reaction to my own stupidity, I hear him gently tap on the door.

"Are you okay, Laurie?"

I bite my lip and shake my head, suppressing another bout of laughter at my current situation. "Yeah, sorry, I'll be out in a sec," I tell him.

"O-kay." His tone is unsure, but I breathe out a sigh after I hear him walk away.

Once my feet move me back into the living room, and I see Ruben is standing, waiting for me, I let myself relax some, but I'm still scared to touch anything in his showcase house. I'm pretty sure I'd have to sell my body, for at least three years, to be able to pay for anything should I break it. Ruben walks out of the room and I stand still, not sure what I'm supposed to do.

"Do you want a drink?" His deep voice comes from what I assume is the kitchen, and there seems to be an invisible cord making me take a few steps in that direction. Just as I reach the door, Ruben walks back around. "Did you hear…" The words die in his throat as he nearly bangs into me. I find my nose almost touching his Henley wrapped chest, and as I let my head fall back so I can see his eyes, my chin grazes the material which sends an unwanted shiver down my back. "Sorry," he whispers, reaching his hand out and cupping my elbow. Not that I was going anywhere, my body seems to be magnetized to his.

I break the moment. "Coffee." My voice is croaky.

"What?" he asks.

"Drink... you asked what I wanted to drink. Coffee please," I rush out.

His fingers peel away from my elbow, and I can feel the singe that he's left behind. Deciding I'm better off giving us some distance, I ask, "Is it okay if I go sit in back in there," pointing back to the living room.

"Of course," he replies. His voice is gravelly, and although I haven't been with anyone for a while, I still know that sound, and I can't help the smirk that forms knowing I've affected him. Walking back into the other room, I take a seat and fidget, unsure of how to sit or what to do. My legs are restless, so I slip off my shoes and tuck my feet under me. Thoughts run through my head as I realize the automatic movement I just made, something which I've never done in anyone's home other than my own. It's a comfort thing.

"It's okay, I want you to be comfortable," Ruben says, rounding the corner with two cups of coffee, and scaring the crap out of me at the same time. I look up to his eyes as his tall frame bends at the waist placing the cup on the small table in front of me.

How could he have possibly known what was running through my head?

"Tell me about you, Ruben." I'm surprised the minute the words leave my lips. Even though Ruben used to come to my groups, he never really said much about what happened, or how he felt. He always seemed like he was haunted. Whoever he did speak to, if anyone, that person certainly wasn't me. Danny gave me some basic background information, but not much. He was engaged and she died from cancer. A great love story, one with an unhappy ending. Leaving behind a man so in love with a woman, who's now only a memory. I'm realistic, I can't compete with her, and I'm never going to try. Suddenly, I feel very cold and uncomfortable. I'm not sure anymore why I allowed him to bring me here, to take me anywhere actually. This is all the result of a silly crush that I have on an unobtainable man.

"You know I lost Amanda." Ruben's words break me from the spiral I was edging toward, and I release a stuttering breath. Closing my eyes slowly and swallowing, I can almost feel his pain, like it exists as its own being. "Laurie," Ruben speaks softly and I feel his fingers graze my arm.

Opening my eyes the first thing I see is his smile. It's sad, but not broken like it was before. This is where I can see the change in him. He used to be so obviously broken, that I didn't know if he would ever get past it. When he disappeared from my life, I worried that he had become a statistic, that he would lose his life either to the drink, living day by day consumed by alcohol, or maybe even lose his life in the literal sense. It amazes me that this is the same man. His progress is something he should be proud of, yet understanding how it feels to lose someone you love, I know that pride in getting over their death is not something I'd want as my accomplishment.

Remembering he said my name I reply, "What?"

"It's okay." I'm unsure what he's trying to convey, so I tilt my head slightly. Ruben takes in my movement and stares for a few moments, before matching my stance, tilting his head until it's aligned with mine. "I used to hate talking about her. For two reasons. One, because it reminded me, and although she was on my mind all the time, it seemed to hurt more when I let out the words. Secondly, because I felt that no one deserved her story. Nobody was good enough including myself, I didn't deserve to speak her name." With our heads still tilted, I bite my lip and slowly straighten my body back up.

Ruben does the same, then points between the two of us. "I used to feel like that."

I can feel my eyebrows pull inwards as the confusion makes my brain fuzzy. "You've lost me… feel like what?" I question.

"Like my world was tilted." His response rocks me. The slanting of our heads is symbolic for him. I can't think on it too long before he explains, "I always felt like my life was off. I've never been able to put my finger on it just that something was missing. I had a thriving company, good friends and a full life. I also had no problem finding women." He watches me, measuring my reaction to his comment, but I bite back anything I feel. I'm not entitled to let a small comment hurt me, I'm not even sure if he's my friend, so I definitely have no claim on him, or his previous life.

When he seems satisfied he continues with his story, "I was friends with Danny, but we both left our hometowns behind, along with women we had cared about. It was Anabel for Danny, he left her even though he loved her. I had always liked Amanda, I'd wanted to take things further, but something always stopped me pursuing her." He shakes his head with a smirk. "Danny went back after years of being away and he met up with Anabel. Around that time, Amanda had come back from Paris, which is where she'd lived for ten years."

My heart thumps in my chest. I'm torn, amazed and elated that he's opening up, but scared shitless, because I don't want to know more about her. From what I picked up when I was last in his life she already sounds amazing. My thoughts are cut off quickly.

"Danny and Anabel soon became a couple again. Amanda and me had a natural connection. I'm not going to lie, I loved her. I was going to marry her."

There it is. I knew this basic information about him, but somehow hearing it come from his lips, makes it feel like he's piercing me with every word.

"She wasn't meant to be my forever though."

I catch my breath. "She could have been." The sentence involuntarily leaves my brain and travels to my mouth, spewing out with no filter applied.

"She could have been." He echoes my thoughts back to me. I nod but say nothing, instead looking down at my clasped hands. "I hated her." At his confession my eyes snap back to his. He nods, as though he needs to confirm what he just said. "I did. I hated her. She left me and I blamed her for it… for something she had no control over." He sighs and opens his arms, laying them on the back of the sofa as he sits facing me. "Dick move, right? I just couldn't see past the fact that *I* was the one suffering, *I* was the one in pain. It was all about *me.* I'm serious as shit when I say that if Amanda were here, she would have kicked me in my junk for behaving that way." He smirks, but it drops from his face quickly as his eyebrows draw in. "The thing with Amanda and me, and I feel like a piece of shit for saying this, but over the time I've spent in rehab and when I opened up to a counsellor, it made me re-evaluate everything. I will never say I didn't love Amanda, because I did, and to deny that would be disrespectful and would also make me a dick. But I wonder, would we have stayed together if she didn't have cancer?" Ruben shoots up out of his seat so quickly that I jump at his movement. He strides to the window and looks up at the stars which are now covering the dark sky. "I hate myself for saying it, but Simpson…" he stops and looks at me, "…my counselor." I nod and he turns back to the stars. "He said that if you took away the cancer would you still have been with Amanda. Yes. The answer was immediate. Then he asked, 'If she didn't have cancer, do you think you would have had a future? Could you see yourself with her forever?'"

He brings his arm up and thumps the wall next to the window. "The honest answer is I don't know. That was a shit storm to face. It gave me lots of hours in that fucking room with Simpson, and really tested my strength when it came to avoiding alcohol. Amanda and I never got together when we were teenagers, we had a chemistry, but never took it further. The minute I saw her again, before I knew about the illness, the chemistry was right there. I wonder if we would have always had a fast and hard relationship. That brief love that gives us a small taste of bigger things to come, the kind that teaches us the meaning of the word. One which had a time limit. We were both too alike. Impulsive, controlling, determined... and not always in a good way."

He smirks at me and the ball in the pit of my stomach starts unfurling. "We were so similar that I think we would have had an expiration date, no matter the cause. So I did love her, a part of me always will. I'll never regret what I had with her, and her loss, it knocked me sideways. But I'm in a place now where I think of my past fondly, warm thoughts and feelings. Memories I can smile at rather than feel pain. I know how it feels when you pass that point, when you climb over that last hurdle, when you get to that place where you're ready to move on."

I catch my breath as Ruben stares at me. I find myself wondering, even hoping, maybe he's trying to tell me that he could see himself moving on with me. Then he knocks me back down, without even realizing it. "I want to help you get over that last hurdle, I can see you're not past it. Give me a chance, then one day you can move forward in your life, meet someone, have a family of your own. Release yourself from your past."

I feel my stomach drop, but my body betrays me as I nod my head in agreement.

"Okay," I say quietly. I'm not sure if I just want to spend more time with Ruben, or if this is going to be the first step to the release I so desperately need. The freedom that for five years, I've denied myself.

An alarm beeps in the kitchen, breaking the tension that I know, at least partly, is caused by me. Thoughts are running through my head one after another. I replay his words, the help he wants to give me, and the fact that it seems as though I'm not what he wants, despite the way he's been acting toward me.

"Sorry..." Ruben returns, cutting into my thoughts, "...I was going to cook something." He stops and rubs the back of his neck. "Yeah, the thing is… I put the timer on, but forgot to put the food in the oven." His announcement coupled with the confused look on his face makes me laugh. I find it's therapeutic and loosens all the worry. By the time I've calmed down, I notice Ruben is still standing in the same place, now with a look of something… wonder maybe? He gazes at me, and I decide to wrap up the rest of my concern into a neat little package to be analyzed another time.

"Shall I order pizza?" I offer still smiling.

Ruben nods handing me the phone. "I like having you here, Laurie," he says nothing more and I smile, realizing nothing else is needed as I relax and know that I'm just going to enjoy a nice night with my friend. Not looking into it any more than that... for now.

Chapter TWELVE

Ruben

"You done?" Danny asks, throwing the towel across his shoulders. I look up to him from my seated position. Having just spent two hours in the gym after slacking off for the last few weeks, I've forgotten how hard Danny pushes, not only himself but others too. He came from a sports background, was in the NFL and if it weren't for an injury, he'd still be the superstar football player. I was never able to keep up, nothing's changed as we've gotten older, but I can still hold my own.

Smiling up at him, I nod. "Yeah man, two hours and my arms are dead. I'd forgotten what a Pitbull you were with training."

Danny gulps some water down his throat and then looks back to me. "You're getting soft, it's only been three weeks, you can't be that tired. I'm thinking it's a certain petite brunette that has you distracted, meaning you're not putting one hundred percent in." He smirks at me. "Don't think I can't see how your focus is off. You normally go all out. Since you've been spending time with Laurie, you've missed more gym sessions than you've attended and you have this faraway look, like a pubescent teen." He chuckles and I throw my towel at his head.

"Fuck you," I push out through a grin, then stand up as he passes me back my towel. We walk out to the changing rooms in silence, heading off to have our showers.

"So you do really like her then?" Danny asks once we've showered, dressed, and are packing up our bags.

Stopping what I'm doing, I look up at him. "Yeah." This is the first time I've really allowed myself to say it, with meaning. I'm not stupid, I've admitted to myself that I like her. More than that, my feelings are growing all the time. Opening up the day I took her back to my apartment for food proved to be the biggest turning point. She still has to talk to me about what happened to her, the demons of the past are still very much alive and clawing the inside of her soul. I'm hoping to change that, but it's going to take time, and that's something I have in abundance lately. But even if I didn't, for her I'd find the time. She's fragile and I'm treading carefully... for now.

"Have you told her?" he asks and I pull in my eyebrows at the odd question.

"Why would you ask that?" I reply.

As we reach the cars, he pulls his trunk open and throws in his bag. "I know you. She's damaged."

In the middle of opening the door to my truck, I stop, turning to face him. "What are you saying?" I ask, the question is low and growled out, which surprises me.

Danny doesn't seem as bothered by the warning tone in my voice and just chuckles shaking his head. "Listen, Ruben. I didn't mean anything by it, I just worry about you."

I throw the bag into my truck and fold my arms over my chest.

Danny smirks. "I didn't want you to like her just because you want to *fix her*." He holds up his hands, which stops me telling him to get fucked. "I have no problem with you fixing her—"

"Thanks for your approval," I cut him off.

"I was worried about you both. You've been so much better. I know you're ready for a new relationship. Well, as ready as you're ever gonna be."

He pulls in his eyebrows and looks at his feet, as though he's struggling with something.

"Spit it out," I tell him and his eyes snap back to mine. Now they're all business.

"I'm worried you won't be able to fix her, and that you'll end up being hurt more. Or, the other side would be, you fix her, then you leave her, and she breaks completely. Right now she has a structure to her life, she's coping, surviving. If you break her, you'll take those tools away."

I pull my hand down my face. "What the fuck are you talking about?" I snap out.

"Listen, you aren't going to like this, but try to get what I'm saying. It's not that I think you will *ever* purposely hurt her. It's just, you haven't been interested in anyone since Amanda..." he pauses and the throb is still there, but it's not a sharp pain anymore, just a memory of someone who I still miss. "Suddenly, you see Laurie again after all this time. It just seems coincidental that she's going through the motions of life, and although you've been around her before, there was never a spark. Now there is?"

He shakes his head. "Sorry, I know you hate me interfering with your shit, but you know that's *never* stopped me before, and I ain't about to start now. I don't want her to be your project. You fell in love with Amanda and I'm not saying it wasn't real, but part of it had to have been the situation. You can't tell me that you would have married her that quickly otherwise?"

I swallow the bile in my throat, knowing how true his words are and it's killing me. "I'm just worried, if you fix Laurie, giving her your time, your strength, your love... by giving her those things, you're giving her *you*. Then when she's fixed and you think you can leave... you won't be looking in your rear view mirror at someone who's been fixed. You won't even be looking at someone who's once again broken. If you fix her, then leave... you'll be looking back at someone you've destroyed."

We stand in silence for a few moments while I contemplate his words. "I like her, okay? Not just to *fix* her." The rumble of words shows the anger inside. I know that he's coming from a good place, and I love him, but *fuck* he pisses me off sometimes.

"All right. I'll shut up," he says with a smirk.

"Fuck you, dick," I reply, but I'm over the annoyance already. "I like her. I never thought about her in that way before. Hell, I never thought about her *at all* before. Back then, you know my world was black. I would've been over Amanda a long time before if it wasn't for the alcohol... and trust me, that shit is hard to say. Somewhere in here..." I thump my chest over my heart, "...I feel like I'm betraying her by not being so broken all the time. I was exhausted, man. So fucking tired of always feeling numb or in pain. I've let it go, and now I know what I want. Right now, I'm offering her friendship. She's taken it and we've become close. I'd be a lying bastard if I said I don't see how fucking amazing she is. I can't push it, though, or her. Not yet."

"Meaning you will at some point?" he asks.

"Only for so long. I can't last looking at her, spending time with her, smelling her and not being able to touch her," I explain.

"Yeah, you don't sound like much of a creeper," Danny tells me with a smirk.

"Fuck off, you fucker," I reply. "Go on, get back to your family. Say hi to Anabel," I tell him before getting into my car. Reversing out of the space, Danny taps on my roof before I can drive away. I open my window for him.

"For what it's worth… she's fucking perfect for you, man. This time, you could have it all."

I don't reply. Just raise my chin in the affirmative and drive away, hoping I'm strong enough to bring us both into the light. Then, maybe, Laurie might be the future I never thought I'd have.

Chapter Thirteen

Laurie

"You've been really quiet lately. More than usual. What's going on?" Sarah asks, gazing at me from over her coffee.

Frowning, while blowing the steam from my cup, I think about my response. "I have a lot on my mind." It's the truth. I know that won't appease her, but I don't want to get into everything right now. Although, I have a feeling I'm not going to escape at least part of it.

"Um-hum," she replies, raising one perfectly arched eyebrow back at me.

"I've been spending time with Ruben."

"I've noticed," she answers grinning.

Shaking my head, I sip the coffee before returning it to the table. "No. Not like that. I don't think he sees me in *that* way." My eyes widen as I realize what I've just admitted out loud.

"But you want him to." It's not a question, Sarah can read me so well.

I hang my head. "I liked him. Back then, before, when I was trying to help him. But—"

"He hurt you."

At her statement, my head jerks back up and I give her a small smile.

"He didn't mean to, he was in pain, drunk most of the time, and didn't really have a good grip on his own behavior or his own life," I tell her. She nods at me but says nothing, waiting for me to open up. It's not something I'm good at doing, and even though I've known Sarah for years and she's the closest thing I have to a best friend, I still find myself clamming up and not wanting to be honest. I'm similar with Amber, but then I put that down to the fact that I see Amber like a daughter. The only person I've been able to open up to easily, sometimes without even meaning to is Ruben. Which is stupid, because I know Sarah so much better. There's just something so comforting about him. And lately, I find I'm immediately at ease in his company.

"I know. There's no judgment here. You know that, Laurie."

"Yeah." I sigh. "I know."

"So how have things been?" Sarah grabs our empty cups and walks over to the sink, washing each one. I maneuver myself next to her and rest my hip against the cupboard.

"I've actually had such a good time with him. He's a genuinely lovely man." I can't help the smile that spreads across my face. "After the first night when I ate at his place, we've gone out to eat, just to the diner but it was great. He took me rock climbing."

"But you don't like heights."

Laughing I reply, "I know! He learned that when we arrived. He also found out that I don't much like surprises." Sarah giggles back at me. "Then he took me to the zoo."

"Really? Well done him." She slaps her hands together.

"Yeah, I think he was pretty pleased with himself when he saw how much I love animals. Even though, I'm still on the fence about them being kept in a zoo." I frown at that thought then continue, "He makes me smile, Sarah." Grabbing her arm, I lean in. "He makes me feel like I'm important, like I'm worth something."

Sarah wipes at a tear pooling in the corner of her eye. "I'm glad someone is finally getting into that noggin of yours just how special you are."

I drop my arm and my smile. "It hurts, though."

"What does?"

"I'm never going to be able to compete with his ex. No matter what he's told me, I know she meant so much to him, I'm scared I'll just be sloppy seconds." I move over to the seat where we just were and sit back down. "The sad thing is, I'd take sloppy seconds any day with him. If he wanted me, I'd be anything he wished for."

Sarah walks over and crouches down in front of me grabbing my hands in her own. "You do not deserve to be someone else's sloppy seconds, girl. But, I don't think you would be with him. The way I've seen him around here, both with the seniors and with you, he's not the same man who came here all that time ago. He's changed, and Laurie, the way he looks at you when you don't see…" she sucks in a breath through her teeth, "…he doesn't just gaze at you like he's already a man in love, it's not clichéd crap. Not with Ruben. He watches you like he's sure that any minute, you're going to do something extraordinary, and he absolutely doesn't want to miss it."

My mouth opens and closes a few times. I'm stuck, unsure what to say to that, but I don't have to say anything because Sarah carries on, "You may think that he doesn't feel anything for you, but girl, you'd be *wrong*. That man knows what he has in you, he's just biding his time. Trust me. And anyway, anyone who cares about you, and you know I love you girl, can see there's more going on in here." She taps my head. "He has to get in there before you really open up in here." She moves her finger until it hovers over my heart. "My thinking, and if I'm any decent kind of counselor then I'm right, is that once you really let him in, he'll give you the life you deserve filled with tenderness and love."

"You're going to make my eyes puffy," I tell her, smiling through the few tears that have fallen down my face.

"Come here, girl," she says, pulling me into her chest and wrapping her arms around me. I sigh, but it's a happy one. Closing my eyes, I enjoy the moment. I don't have many hugs. That sounds ridiculous to even think, but unfortunately, it's true. Even when Larissa and Rocco were alive—that kid… God that kid—he always had a hug ready for me. But I was always so busy and Larissa wasn't physically able to do much of anything most of the time, the haste of our lives passing us by and the hours I worked, meant I didn't have the small things that we take for granted like hugging.

My parents were always cold. Strict. Absent. I'm not sure why they had Larissa and me if I'm being perfectly honest. We weren't treated like they wanted us, loved us, it was more like they felt it was the right thing to do.

Find an appropriate partner in college. Check.

Wait a suitable amount of time before getting engaged. Check.

Get married. Check.

Buy a house. Check.

Have Children. Check.

There was no thought behind it, and looking back at it all now, I think they were more than relieved when they saw the back of the both of us. Amber gives me hugs when I ask, and I have to ask because she wasn't brought up with love either. So it's an unnatural act for her. I don't want to ask anymore, I just want to be loved, to be able to walk up to someone and slip my arms around them, knowing they'll do the same back to me.

Sarah pulls back and grabs a tissue handing it to me. "So, is he in today?" she asks me.

I shake my head. "No. He went to visit his mom this weekend. He'll be back tonight, and I have tomorrow off..." my voice trails away, not really sure what I'm trying to say.

"So you're hoping he'll call and make plans for tomorrow?" She watches me and I shrug my shoulders in response. "Don't worry girl, he'll call. I'd lay money on it." She winks at me. "Come on, I have a session in ten, and you need to get everything ready for your next meeting. I've seen the office, sheesh. That admin pile never goes down, does it?"

What's Left of Me

I chuckle. "Nope. Come on." I link my arm through hers and we walk back to my office, where she leaves me and heads to hers. I close my door and sit at my desk, unlocking my computer and sitting back in the chair. The photo on my desk of Rocco catches my eye, and I pick it up kissing his little boy face. With emotion still swirling inside of me, it's not long until the tears start again.

"I let you down. I'm not sure I deserve the future Sarah thinks I do. As much as I'd love it. Why should I get that future, when you haven't got yours? It's my fault, baby boy. I killed you." Putting the photo back, I lay my head on the desk. "God, I miss you," I whisper to him.

Ten minutes later I'm still slouched there, wondering how in the hell I'm ever going to beat back the demons, when I belong in hell right along with them.

Chapter Fourteen

Ruben

"The weather was rainy today."

"Yeah, it was Mom."

"It was rainy, I got wet." My mom scratches at her head then picks imaginary lint from her lap.

"You're dry now," I tell her tenderly.

"It was raining. I got wet," she repeats, not looking at me.

Sighing, I flex my hands. *I hate this disease.* She would hate this disease if she knew. Sometimes, I'm thankful she really doesn't know.

"Who are you? Where's my momma? Momma! Momma!" she screeches.

"It's okay, I'm going. Look, I'm leaving. I'll get your momma, okay? Shall I put something on the television to watch?"

"Momma!" she shouts again, but then goes quiet as she watches me move toward the door as I turn the television on for her.

"I'm gonna go," I tell my Aunt Karen.

"Okay, my sweet boy. Don't worry, your mom will be fine, just like usual," she tells me and I nod. I know she's right, my mom doesn't know any better. It's just so hard to watch a woman that was so strong, a woman who raised her only son by herself when my pa died, not have any control over her life anymore. At one point my mom had three jobs, and yet still found time to take me to sports and help me with homework. Now she's so frail, she has no clue who any of us are, or even who *she* is most of the time. It's like she's losing herself from the inside out. I'll never let her down, though. I come visit every other weekend. Sometimes for the whole weekend, sometimes just for a day. I know it's time to leave when she starts asking who I am and getting agitated. It doesn't happen every time, but it's happening more often than not lately.

"Love you, Aunt Karen," I say, pulling her in for a hug. Apart from my mom, she's the only family I still have. She never had kids and my mom and her were the only children. I don't know my pa's family, so here I am, the last in the line.

"I have to say this to you, Ruben. So shut up and listen, okay?"

She surprises me, but I nod and remain quiet.

"I'm proud of you. You've pulled yourself up, exorcised your demons, gotten on with your life, you haven't been weak."

I want to argue, to say that I was weak, for years I let myself be controlled by drink and grief, but I know there's no point. She wants to say this, so I'm going to let her.

"I was so scared when you started spiraling. I thought we were going to lose you. I thought it would just be Rosina and me." She nods toward my mom. "I love you." She reaches up and cups my cheek, in the way only an auntie can. Automatically I lean down to her small five-foot frame and allow her to kiss my cheek.

"I know." I straighten up and grab my bag, heading out the door to my truck. It's an hour's drive to my apartment, and for some reason, I just don't want to go there. Once I'm on the freeway, I call up the voice control on my cell, check it's connected to the speaker system and make the call I need to hear the one voice that soothes my soul.

"Ruben?" I close my eyes, but just for a split second, so as not to cause an accident.

What's Left of Me

"Laurie," I breathe out her name and even I can hear the relief in my voice.

"Are you okay?" she asks, worry evident in her tone.

"Yeah, sorry. I've just had a hard time at my mom's this weekend. I really don't want to go home. How would you feel about me coming over to yours for a bit?" I ask the question. She can say no. Over the last three or so weeks, we've spent a lot of time together, I've picked her up from her apartment, but I've never been inside. She's kept me away and I haven't pushed, not until now. There's only so long that I'm going to tiptoe around the situation. I want Laurie to release herself from whatever shit she keeps wrapped up inside. I also want her to be mine.

Slowly I'm slipping into a friendship with her, which is fine, but I'm not going to be friend zoned. So I need to stop this shit before it gets too far. This woman has me seeing my future in a different color than I ever have before. Twelve months ago and that thought would have made me ashamed of myself. Now I realize it's okay to move on. I know Amanda told me to, but doing it is a different thing altogether. There's one thing that still makes me feel a little sour, it's that I could see myself loving Laurie more than I ever did Amanda.

"Sure, c-come over," Laurie stutters and I feel like a douche for forcing the issue.

"Listen, Laurie, it's okay, I'm sorry for pushing. If you want, I could pick you up and we could go to the diner," I offer half-heartedly, hoping she can hear something in my voice that tells her I want to be in her space.

"No," she snaps and I open my mouth not sure what to say when she continues, "Sorry, I mean, no, come over, it's fine. Just… just remember it's not like your place, okay?" I can hear the worry in her voice, and I hate that she feels that way.

"You know me better than that, babe. I'll be there in forty," I tell her.

"Okay. Bye Ruben," she whispers and it hits me in my chest and dick. She disconnects and I let my head roll back while still keeping my eyes on the road.

"Shit. I'm fucked."

Forty-five minutes later and I'm parked and jogging up the steps to her apartment, noting that the security door was unlocked. Before I get a chance to knock her apartment door is flung open and Laurie stands in the entrance. My eyes take her in. Her chocolate hair falls in soft natural waves over her shoulders. She has what looks like yoga pants on, and a plain blue V-necked top. She has no make-up on, and I love that she's comfortable in her own skin. It's her eyes and lips that always take my breath away, though. Her eyes are such a bright green, it's like looking into a crystal clear ocean, and her lips are full and so fucking kissable.

"Ruben." Her soft voice is too much this time, and with my arm still on her door surround, I lean my body down and place my lips on hers. At first, she's frozen, but within a second, I feel her melt into me, and that's when I bring my arm down and wrap it around her back. I kiss her softly at first, but when I feel her hands move up my chest, fisting in my top as she nips my lip I lose some of my control. Bringing my hand up, I thread my fingers into her hair and gently tug her head back, allowing me more access. I pull away slightly and kiss the corner of her mouth. She opens her lips and her eyes are wide, I lean back in and capture her once again letting my tongue enter. It's been years since I've kissed a woman, but I'm not sure anyone has ever had this effect on me. I bring both my hands down to her butt, and while still kissing her, I lift her whole body up. She gasps as I push her against the wall, but I don't give her a chance to say anything, as I claim her mouth again. She brings her legs up and wraps them around my waist and I groan down her throat.

Laurie pulls away from me slightly, looking into my eyes. I take in her thoroughly kissed lips, swollen and red, and I feel myself aching to do more than just kiss this woman. Slowly, hesitantly, she lifts her fingers and presses them against my lips. Her eyes are glued to what she's doing, then suddenly her eyes snap back to mine.

"Ruben," she whispers my name once again, and I wonder if this is the way it's going to be for the rest of my life. All she'll ever have to do is whisper my name for me to lose all control with her.

"Fuck. I think you might be made for me," I murmur and watch as her mouth hangs open. I take that as my cue and kiss her again, knowing I'm not going to get enough of this woman. I'm not sure I'll ever have enough.

Chapter Fifteen

Laurie

My senses filter in as Ruben continues claiming my mouth. His kisses are something else, it's like this is going to be the last time he's ever going to experience a woman's lips. Or maybe I've just never been kissed like this before, like I'm his air like his survival depends solely on me.

"Ah-hum," I hear Amber cough from the doorway. I close my eyes as I feel Ruben look around me.

"Hey. You must be Amber." His voice is strong and doesn't waver, even though he still has me hoisted up against the wall. I tap his shoulder and bring his attention back to me. It's only then that he releases me and I slide down the wall until my unsteady feet hit the floor.

"Yeah, I'm Amber." She smirks then walks into the kitchen.

"Give me a minute?" I ask Ruben, he nods while tucking my hair behind my ear. It's such an intimate gesture, something he's only done once before, that I'm stuck for a second.

"Go. I'll wait in the living room," he says walking to the opposite door that Amber just disappeared through.

When I enter the kitchen, I'm not sure what to expect. Amber has always been anti-Ruben, and although she was just smirking, I'm worried. However, I find she's dancing against the kitchen counter, while making a peanut butter and jelly sandwich, seemingly like she hasn't got a care in the world, bopping her head while her earphones ruin her hearing. I walk up behind her and pull the right one out of her ear.

She spins around. "Hey, what you doing?" Her eyebrows are pinched, and I'm left slightly stunned.

"I thought you'd want to talk, you know, about out there," I say pointing to the front door.

"Oh, not really." She squirms and I cross my arms.

"Look, a month ago you were telling me to stay away from him, you were completely against everything Ruben. You cannot possibly tell me you've done a one-eighty? I mean, I know teens are shallow and wishy-washy with their opinions, but that's never been you," I tell her something she knows.

"I've been watching you." Her answer isn't what I'm expecting and so I have no reply. "He's been coming to the center. You know... there have been times where I've been there too. At first, I couldn't believe for even a second that he was somehow now interested in you. I figured he needed to have a cheerleader, someone in his corner telling him what a clever boy he was. Then I spoke to Sarah. She explained how he'd been with you, how you light up when he's around." She shrugs her shoulders. "I paid attention. To the both of you. You've been different lately, Laurie... a good different. You're happier in general. He does something to you, and by what I just saw out there, you do the same thing to him." She turns to continue making her sandwich. "Anyway, I've changed my mind about him... woman's prerogative," she says throwing a grin over her shoulder. Then she spins around again with the knife in her hand. Waving it about, she finishes with, "If he hurts you again, though, I will not be responsible for what appendage I'll cut off. Remember, I'm off to study medicine."

"Okay, *Rambo*," I say shaking my head with a grin. I lean over and kiss her forehead. "Love you, girlie," I tell her.

"You too, Laurie," she replies before turning back to her food and popping the earphone back in. "I'm going to Judd's house," she throws out before walking away.

I eye her up and down as she walks out of the apartment, then sigh. Judd is a guy who she's been friends with for a couple of years, but I'm pretty sure she has a big ole crush on him and I worry. But she's eighteen and going off to college soon… with Judd. I need to let her fly free.

When I walk into the living room, I'm struck by how comfortable Ruben looks. Spread out on the sofa, even though it's miles too small for his large frame, he still looks like that's right where he belongs.

"Hey you," I say softly, unsure of what I'm supposed to do. A million things are rattling through my brain, and I can't pin down any one thought.

"Hey, come here." He pats the space next to him and I sink down. Lying his arm across the back of the sofa, he turns to look at me.

"What?" I say shyly, turning my head and catching his eyes.

"Don't be coy, Laurie," he says, smirking.

"Douche," I reply with a smile.

What's Left of Me

"You have to know I've wanted to kiss you for weeks now." His words make all the air rush out of my lungs. "Don't look so shocked. I know how I've seemed in the past and I already told you I'm sorry. I'm not going to keep going over that shit, even though I truly am sorry. I never noticed you before, because I never noticed *anyone*. There was no way I could sift through the shit that I had swirling around up here," he says digging his index finger into his temple. "You're special, Laurie, in more ways than one. And now I know you can fucking kiss, too." I giggle at his words then cut myself off feeling slightly embarrassed at acting like a schoolgirl. "That right there needs to stop. You can take all the time you need to get over your shit, just understand I'll be here every step of the way, lighting your path."

"You want a drink?" I ask, suddenly aware that I need a minute.

He narrows his eyes on me but lets it go when he answers. "Yeah, what you got?"

My eyes widen when I realize I don't have much. "Errm, instant coffee?" I tell him, biting my lip.

"Sounds good. You got take-out menus? I'll order while you make the coffee," his reply is all business and he completely ignores my embarrassment, which makes me just want to kiss him. *Hard.*

"Yeah," I reply, grabbing them from the pile next to my bills. "Here." I pass them to him and scurry off to the kitchen. Placing my hands on the countertop, I let my head hang down taking some deep breaths. "Just breathe, Laurie," I whisper. The kettle clicks off and I make him the coffee. Staring out the window in front of me, which faces the brick wall of another apartment building, I close my eyes and try to steady myself. I feel lightheaded, knowing Ruben Asher is in my apartment, and he's just kissed me. It's all sinking in and I'm slightly stunned like maybe I dreamt it.

On that thought warmth hits my back. Ruben rests his chin on my shoulder, places his hands on my hips and rumbles in my ear, "Pizza's ordered."

"Okay," I manage to say. He moves his hand down and away catching my fingers and gripping them. Tugging me back to the living room, ignoring the coffee, neither of us says anything as he seats himself then pulls me onto his lap. "Your coffee," I murmur.

"Shhh," he replies as he brings two fingers up to my lips, firstly to silence me, then he uses them to trace my mouth. "You're the most beautiful woman I've ever seen." His words are hushed like he's not saying them to me. My stomach has butterflies, and I feel like I want to both cry with happy tears and kiss his face off. There's no choice to be made, when he leans in and touches my mouth with his again. This time, I automatically open, allowing his tongue entry.

What's Left of Me

As his hands move down across my body, I pull away. I need to know where this is going. I know he said that he'd wanted to kiss me for ages, and that he was going to be lighting my path as I battled my way through the issues I still harbor, but he has no idea what he's letting himself in for and I'm not ready to tell him—*yet*. But, I do need to know what this is, what he wants.

"Ruben," I whisper his name as I pull away and he growls low.

"The way you say my name, it drives me crazy." He moves down, kissing my neck and I allow my head to flop backward, the pleasure overtaking me. Dragging my will together as best I can, I push him off me.

"We need to talk," I say softly.

He looks at my face, and something he sees must register as he nods immediately, sitting back.

"What… w-what is this?" I ask waving a finger between us.

His eyes narrow and he looks annoyed, it's not what I expected from him, but then his anger is explained when he starts speaking. "We've been spending time together these last few weeks," he tells me and I nod. "You've gotten to know me pretty well…." he continues and I nod again, "…have I mentioned anybody since Amanda?" I shake my head. "In fact, I'm pretty sure that I told you I haven't been with anyone since her, being too wrapped up in my own shit to even notice women… until you. We've become pretty good friends, yeah?"

I bite my lip, this time, worried about how upset he seems. His eyes move to my lip then back to my eyes. Sighing, he moves me onto the seat next to him and I instantly feel cold as my stomach clenches.

His voice is softer when he continues talking, "Look, we've been getting closer. You're the first person I've kissed in so long. I wouldn't ruin this friendship we've built up if I didn't think what we have could be something special. Something that was worth pursuing. Something that could possibly be forever…" I gasp at his words. "Yeah, see *that's* where I'm at." He nods but it's with sadness.

Timidly, I reach my hand out and grab hold of his arm. "I really like you, I'm sorry if you took offense to me asking, but I had to know. I haven't had a boyfriend or even a kiss in so long, it's been—"

He cuts my rambling off. "I really don't want to know about your history. The only thing I would want to know was if you were a virgin. Otherwise, let's not hash out the past conquests."

I stare at him for a good few seconds.

"Oh God, are you a virgin?" he asks, his own eyes now almost popping out of his head.

"No, no, I'm not." I smirk, pulling my lips in-between my teeth as his whole body relaxes.

"What is it that you're worried about? I can sense there's something. We need to hash it out now, Laurie. Otherwise, whatever this could be, is never going to get past this point right here." His voice is low, and I feel a frisson of excitement and nervousness run through my body.

"It's your past, it's Amanda." The words are expelled in one go like I can't breathe until they're out of my body. The instant they are out, in the open, Ruben goes still and I'm not sure whether I've fucked everything up by allowing myself to be honest with him. Even if I have, though, I know unless we discuss her, this issue will always be between us, in the way of whatever we could have.

"Come again?" he asks.

I close my eyes, already knowing I've fucked this whole thing up. I may as well be honest with him now. "You loved her, and you didn't split up. It wasn't like you fell out of love and went your separate ways. She died…" I whisper the last two words, allowing my eyes to travel to Ruben, but he's staring out into the distance, and I'm not even sure he's hearing me right now. "I saw you, remember? I saw how desperately sad your life became, and how devastated you were. I saw you at your worst. You don't hit that spiral unless the person you lost meant everything to you, the kind of everything that can never be replaced. I thought that I was willing to be second best, just to be with you. I've more than liked you since I met you all those years ago."

I feel Ruben move, but ignore him to carry on. "I was willing to be the runner up to the person you really wanted, knowing I'd never compete with a ghost. But honestly, Ruben, I just don't think I have the strength to always be second guessing myself. And I also think I have enough self-respect to want someone who wants me more than anyone else."

It's when I stop talking and look back to Ruben, I see his eyes have turned liquid hot and there's something animalistic behind them.

He moves so his face is almost touching mine, then he speaks and when he does our lips brush with every word. "Every possible future I can think up, in any reality, containing any people *dead or alive* I still see you. *Me and You*. You're all I see," he says and I feel the emotion creep across my body as he kisses me again. This time closed mouth, soft, gentle touches. Slowly owning every part of me, while only touching one.

Chapter Sixteen

Ruben

My hands move of their own accord, and I quickly pull back before Laurie ends up under me naked. I want nothing more right now, and it takes everything within me to calm down. If I go much further, I won't be able to stop. Five years is a long time to go without sex. First, though, I need to make sure her head is on straight where we're concerned.

"Laurie," I say her name, watching as her eyes open. Her face is flushed, her hair ruffled by my fingers and her lips swollen. I try not to swallow my tongue and instead focus on getting things clear with us. "I know I said I haven't been with a woman for years, but before that, apart from Amanda, I didn't do relationships, I've never wanted one." Her eyes sparkle as the green stands out like a beacon pulling me in. "I figured when I met *the one*, I'd know and that's when I'd want to have a relationship. So here we are, I've met you and I want a relationship." Hoping that my explanation goes some way to convince her and help sort out her head.

I'm surprised when, with a worried look on her face she says, "What about Amanda? You must have thought she was the one?" Her eyes dart to the side, looking away.

"Look at me, Laurie," I demand and her eyes travel back to mine. "Loving Amanda *first*, doesn't mean that I love you *second*. Do you understand what I'm saying?"

Laurie's eyes widen. "You're saying that you love me?" she gasps out.

I'm momentarily stunned into silence. I didn't connect what was coming out of my mouth to my brain. I spoke from my heart, and now that I've said it I understand what I'm feeling inside. These last few weeks, getting to know Laurie better, really seeing inside her, meeting the people she cares about and being around her almost every day, it's happened so gradually that I never noticed. But now there isn't a damn thing I can do about it. I'm too far gone. I can't and don't want to take those words back.

"Yeah. That's exactly what I'm saying," I reply.

What's Left of Me

She climbs onto my lap, straddling me. "I've lived so much of my life in the past. There are still issues I need to face. I'm trying, really I am… but it's slow going, Ruben. There's always been an attraction to you for me. When you came back, I thought we were going to do round two, and I wasn't sure I could face what I went through with you last time." I open my mouth to speak, but she places a slender finger against my lips. Which I promptly suck into my mouth. She gulps, her eyes trained on my mouth and I almost chuckle. If she can straddle me after I've just told her I love her, then it's on.

Fixed in place, her eyes watching her finger, I let it go. "You were saying?" She jerks at my words, rubbing her hips against me in the process and I almost groan.

"Oh, y-yeah. We've spent a lot of time together, and I've gotten to know you, too. You amaze me and obviously I think you're gorgeous."

I grin with satisfaction at her words.

"But there are a lot of gorgeous men out there."

My face falls and I raise my eyebrows, which causes a smile to spread across her face. She absolutely takes my breath away.

"Over this last month or so, you've opened up." She places her flat palm against my chest. "I doubt you allow many people in there. But you've let me in."

"You crawled under my skin, past all my barriers," I tell her.

"I could say the same about you. This is what I want. *You* are what I want. I just had to ask, I had to know that you weren't living in the past, that I would be enough. I never want you to forget your past, just as I'll never forget mine. I just needed to know that you wanted me, loved me... just for me." She smiles through her words this time and I run my hand around the back of her head, pulling her face to mine.

"Just you. It's only you." This time, she devours my mouth as soon as the words leave me. I run my hands up the inside of her top and slip it over her head, breaking our kiss. She looks down at her chest then mine, her eyes hooded. Biting her lip she tugs at my top and I reach over my head and grab it from my back. Throwing my top to one side, I notice Laurie's eyes have widened. She stares at my chest and I can't help the chuckle that escapes.

"I've been working out for a long time. I have nowhere else to expel my energy... well, not until now. This is the result." A frown mars her face as she bites her lip. "What?" I ask, concerned at the turn of emotions.

Her eyes flick to me. "Seeing this..." she says touching my right pec, "...in all its glory, and now knowing it's the result of not having sex, I'm not sure whether I want to have sex, in case you expend all your energy and the gym visits stop."

I belt out a laugh at her comments, but soon stop, watching her tits bounce up and down with my movements. It's too much and I know my control just snapped. Growling, I reach around her and unclasp her bra, pulling it down her arms and chuck it across the room. Glancing at her face for a second, which seems suspended in wonder, I run my tongue over her nipple before seizing it in my mouth. Laurie's head drops back with a low moan and it hits me deep in my gut, sending shivers of anticipation through me. Taking my time, moving from one breast to the other, playtime is over when she runs her hand down my chest and grips my dick through my jeans.

With a loud growl I stand up, taking her with me. Once again in my arms, she wraps her legs around my waist. There's no way she can't feel the monster erection that's digging into her heat. She leans forward into me, sucking my neck as I walk back out the doors and down the small hallway, going to the only one that's closed. Seeing it's slightly ajar, I kick at the bottom and it opens, revealing a bedroom. Twisting, I boot the door closed then take the two strides separating me from the double bed before dropping her gently on her back. I waste no time in removing both her pants and the rest of my clothing.

Now I'm standing there naked, my dick is at full height, so ready to slip into her that a few drops of pre-cum dribble out. I can't move, though. I just stare at probably the sexiest creature I've ever seen. Her whole body has a natural tan. She's small, dainty, slender, and is wearing a pair of black panties with a thin layer of lace around the top. Moving forward, I slip them down her legs. Her cheeks heat at my slow moments.

"I'm taking my time, because once I'm inside you, I won't last long. Not this first time," I explain with a wicked grin, and her hooded eyes flash with awareness then she grins. I place both hands on her ankles and push them apart, moving up her body. My hands slide up the inside of her thighs, continuing to push them apart as I go. Leaning low, I occasionally nip, suck and lick her body. Laurie's eyes are glued to mine, and I smile as I lean over her center and let my tongue travel across her, inside her, around her. Sucking her clit into my mouth, and slipping two fingers deep into her.

Fuck she's tight. It doesn't take long to bring her to the edge. Before she crashes over, I pull away and she whimpers. Smiling, I know in the future, this woman will be getting it from me more than once each time. Tonight, though, there's no way I'd be able to hang on so she could orgasm again. I move over her, letting the tip of my dick rub against her folds.

"Do you have a condom?" I ask, feeling slightly stupid and hoping she both does have one, but at the same time she doesn't.

"Err… no," she whispers squeezing her eyes tightly.

"Shit. I never planned this, I don't carry them anymore. Fuck." I let my head drop forward, knowing I'm going to have blue balls.

"I'm on the pill." She shrugs one shoulder. "Always have been, since Larissa got pregnant." She stops talking and I move to take her mouth with mine, kissing her, covering her with my own version of a balm.

"Are you sure you want to do this? I mean we both know we're clean, but I can wait, Laurie."

She doesn't respond verbally, instead crossing her legs over my butt and urging me toward her. I kiss her mouth again then slip into her, right to the hilt.

"Ahhh," I can't help groaning out.

She makes her own moan down my throat as I kiss her again. I continue taking her mouth as I move back and forth. And don't stop as I grind myself down on her. My lips stay on hers as the release washes over her and then me. Collapsing next to her, our lips are still locked.

I pull back and lay my head on her pillow. She turns her face to mirror mine, her cheeks are glowing from post-coital bliss. Her hair messed up. With my dick still inside her, I watch her eyes soft and happy.

"I love you, Laurie," I say quietly.

"I'm so in love with you, Ruben," she replies.

For the first time in so long, I feel whole.

Chapter Seventeen

Laurie

"You working tomorrow?" Amber asks from opposite me.

"Yeah. What are you doing?" I reply, deciding to avoid the elephant in the room, for as long as is humanly possible.

"Checking out a new bookstore with Judd," she answers then shovels a fork full of egg into her mouth. I pick through my own food, not really feeling hungry as my stomach twists uncomfortably.

"You can say it, you know. It's okay to talk about. In fact, it's probably going to be good to get it out, because whether you want it to or not it's going to happen, Laurie." Amber says, sliding her hand across the table and covering my palm. It's an unusual move for her and I know she's worried about me.

Sighing, I push the stiffness from my limbs and turn my hand palm up so I can wrap my fingers around her wrist, mirroring her hold on me. "I know it's happening, I just want to bury my head in the sand. I love you, and even though you've only been living with me for a couple of years, you're my family. I worry about you… that's all," I explain, swallowing down the prickly emotion climbing up my throat.

"Laurie," she says my name and I look back at her, into her eyes, blinking away my unshed tears. "You know I love you. I know I don't say things like that very often, but it doesn't make it any less true. You're the only family I've ever really known. You took me in, cared for me, gave me so many things that I couldn't begin to explain, let alone thank you for. Now it's your time. You have a good thing at the center. You know that you've got a great chance of taking over Derick's position when he leaves later this year. Plus, there's Ruben. You've had your life on hold for years. Now it's your time, grab it with both hands."

"When did you become the grown up?" I ask with a smirk, trying to cover the mixture of sadness and pride that's running through my veins.

"I learnt the wisdom I possess from you, oh great one… now the student has become the master," she tells me with a wink and then pulls back, the deep discussion forgotten as she picks up her fork and digs back into her eggs with gusto.

It's been six weeks since Ruben and I admitted how we felt. It's not just been six weeks, it's been six amazing weeks. We've talked, laughed, loved and shared our lives, in a way that I never thought would be possible for me. While the time has passed quickly, it's also been full, it's like we've squeezed as much love and enjoyment into each and every moment. Next week will be the first time that Ruben has spent a considerable amount of time away from me. He's returning to work, taking his helm back in a way that he hasn't for years.

On top of that, Amber is heading off to college this weekend. Ruben's helping take her to the dorms. I both hate and love it, all at the same time. I know Amber is right, though, now it's my time. I need to focus on me. She's flying the nest and Ruben is finally pulling his life back together. I love them both, and now I have to make sure I love myself, right?

I move the brush across the wall, coating the dirty gray area with a pastel green. Letting out a little squeak of pride as I take a step back and look at my handy-work. When I first came to the center I wanted to make my mark. The building holds so much possibility, but it's hampered by a gloomy, broken down look that screams depression. I decided it was finally time to brighten this place up. The paint I've stained the walls with isn't much, but it's one step toward my overall goal. We need some funding desperately if the center is going to remain open, but for now, a lick of paint is enough to cheer me up.

"Hey, this looks good," Ruben says, appearing behind me as if by magic. He drops a soft kiss to the corner of my neck and I close my eyes, the happiness spreading through my body like an electrical current.

"Thanks. It's amazing what you can do in just two days," I say wiggling my eyebrows in jest.

"Yeah, one wall. Amazing," Ruben adds dryly, cocking his eyebrow.

"Shut up," I tell him, then turn, touching the tip of his nose with a wet green finger.

"Oh, you want to play that game, huh?" He gives me a wicked grin, and I back up, but it's too late. Lifting me like I weigh nothing, Ruben throws me over his shoulder and fakes to the left, then the right, like he's going to push me against the newly painted wall.

"Okay you two, enough already. I have to put up with this at home, I don't need it here, too," Amber calls out from the doorway. Ruben spins around and as I'm still hanging upside down and pinned against his back, I can't see her. Reaching down to his waist, I rest my hands there, pushing my body sideways, until I'm looking at an upside down Amber. Ruben chuckles and gently lifts me up, before dropping me down. He wraps his arm around my shoulder, bringing me into his side and plants a kiss on my temple, which warms my whole body.

"Nah, I'm kidding. It's good to see you loved up. At least, I know I'm leaving you in safe hands," Amber says looking between the two of us. "Anyway, Judd's picking me up. I'm heading home to pack the last few bits in his truck." Smiling she turns to walk away then stops and twists back around. "You'll be home soon, right?"

The words are offhand, she's trying to mask her feelings, but the shy way she said them, makes her seem like a young girl and not a young woman about to head out into the world on her own. After all these years Amber's still guarded, afraid that she's going to be trodden on. The thought cracks my heart open a bit, but I know my little warrior, she's a survivor and an amazing human being in every way. She taught me that it's okay to care about someone again, it's okay to have family. The new people she lets into her life will be lucky to be so blessed.

"Yeah, we're just finishing up," Ruben tells her with a genuinely warm smile, which makes my heart flutter.

"Okay." Her own smile fills the bottom half of her face. And as always her beauty takes my breath away, I watch with watery eyes, my weakening knees barely holding me up, as she spins back around and dashes off.

"Hey, it will be okay," Ruben soothes, pulling me into him full frontal, holding me up and rubbing up and down my back in long, languid strokes, designed to relax and calm me.

I can't speak, just letting out a mixed up hiccup squeak as I try to contain my sniffles while my stomach is spinning.

"Let's get you home to your girl," he whispers in my ear before we clean up my mess and he bundles me into his truck to deliver me home.

"Come on!" Amber shouts, running up the steps two at a time.

Shaking my head, my mouth smiling while my eyes are desperately trying not to water, I feel Ruben's hand on my lower back. "Let's go, baby."

What's Left of Me

We follow Amber up the stairs and see girls milling about everywhere—parents and boxes in tow. Looking left and right along the corridor, Amber pokes her head out of a doorway. "In here!" she shouts excitedly and I can't help the snort that pops out of my mouth. As we make our way down the long corridor, other girls' moms all eye Ruben appreciatively. It's the first time I've really thought about other women liking him.

When I met him, he was a drunk and too hung up on Amanda to be sleeping with different women. Since he's come back into my life, all his attention has been on me, so even when I've noticed the gazes from females in the past, the thought of another woman wanting him has never seriously crossed my mind. Not until we walked along this corridor. It's like he's a piece of meat on display for them all, that's how they watch him. There's no consideration for me or some of their husbands or kids. Just plain downright rude, ogling.

Prickly heat rushes up over my skin as my eyes narrow, and for a second I'm dumbstruck, wanting to slap someone while threading my arm through his in a claiming gesture. But then I shake my own head at myself. I can't claim him, he has to give himself to me, and he's already done that. The anger dissipates as quickly as it appeared. I can't be with him twenty-four-seven, I can't know what he's always doing, and he's hot. Women are always going to stare. Therefore, I have to trust him, if I can't then I might as well tell him it's over now.

Feeling lighter, having skimmed through my wavering thoughts in less than two minutes, I hit Amber's door, not yet ready to let the beautiful young woman who I see as my own, fly the nest and make her life everything she deserves it to be. Yet, knowing that I'll smile, encourage, and let my heart swell with pride, so she gets everything she needs on, hopefully, the first of many big days in her life to come. All of which I'll get to share with her.

Chapter Eighteen

Ruben

"It's been too long." My throat constricts as I kneel on the damp ground. "I should have come, sat, and spoken to you. There are things I'm sure, even with your silence, you would have told me." Stretching my neck, I wait for the tingling in my hands to stop. I'm not sure if it's from the cold, or my nerves.

I don't know why I'm nervous.

No. That's a lie.

I know why I'm nervous.

I haven't come here since the funeral.

Even though she can't answer me, I know that in spirit she's kicking me repeatedly in the balls. "I haven't been avoiding you. I just…" Pulling my hand down my face, I sigh and watch a puff of white air leave my lips. "Amanda, I spiraled so out of control. I'm pretty sure you would have been ashamed."

Standing up, I pace back and forth, looking at the view of the town I grew up in, from this hill where her grave resides. "It took me so long, so damn long, to get over you, to get over myself. I was completely self-involved. My own pity swallowed me whole for a while." Easing back down on my haunches, I wipe away the leaves that have gathered. I know that Anabel comes here every few months, it's a flight away now she's in New York like me, but Amanda's dad lives in Ireland now. So he only comes back here to celebrate her birthday.

"I made good on my promise," I tell her. "Just after you left us, I checked into him. Pierre. His businesses? The bars he owned, I ripped them all apart. I dismantled his company. Bought it out from under him, called in some favors and spoke directly to the board members." Fidgeting I feel a chill running up my spine, which I want to shake off, but can't because the weather is cutting. "I broke him down. Seems like that company meant everything to him."

I slam my fist on the grave, sudden rage like lava inside me. My muscles clench and unclench repeatedly. "You didn't tell me that you gave him his start, loaning him money because you were married. Money that he never gave you back." Shaking my head I can feel the snake of anger in my stomach uncoiling. "He gave you nothing in the divorce. *Nothing.* I got my guy to look into it. That fucker was going to fight you, wasn't he? He was going to fight his wife when she had cancer. All because he was too chicken shit to deal with it. That low life bastard was going to drag you through court. So you let him have it all."

Raising my coiled body up I take a step away, kicking my foot out and catching a twig, sending it flying through the air. "You wouldn't have wanted his money anyway, I know that. Still, it was a dick thing to do. It just shows what kind of a man he is… which is no man at all." A humorless laugh leaves my mouth as I bite down with irritation. "He lives with his mom now. Works in the local bar. It's the life he deserves. I wanted to do more, but Danny stopped me." I move to sit on the bench, which I paid to have positioned on this path next to her grave. So people could sit and rest. Contemplate. Remember.

I stare at the inscription.

Amanda. Forever my star. Never forgotten.
Eternally loved.

"I'm in love," I say softly, standing back up, unable to stay still. I move to the end of her grave and stare at the roses I placed there.

Amanda loved roses.

Laurie likes tulips.

I don't know why the thought is even in my head, but the moment it's there I feel my automatic smile and my heart picks up speed. Kneeling down again, I lean forward. "I've been with her... Laurie, for a little over six months now. I'm going to ask her to marry me. Not today, maybe not in the next few months. But Amanda, she's it for me."

Clenching my teeth, my stomach tightens. "Danny and Anabel love her. They saw it way before I did, when I was in self-destruct mode and she tried to help me. I know you'd be happy for me, too. You told me to move on. I didn't think I ever would. I knew, though when my head was out of my ass and the alcohol had left my system, the moment I walked out of that rehab center, I just knew I had to go back to her self-help group. It wasn't the group, though."

A wash of emotion passes through my chest, whizzing through my body like a constant hum. "That first meeting, I watched her, before I even really spoke to her. Feelings that I didn't expect to have, and didn't know what to do with, assaulted me from the second I saw her face. When her perfume wrapped around me."

I stop talking as some people walk along the path. We smile and nod politely. Even though this is a smallish town, and people you don't even know often pause to talk, me kneeling on the muddy grass in front of a gravestone gives the '*please leave me alone*' vibe. So they don't stop.

"I freaked out, Amanda. I didn't know what to do with the feelings. Thought I was betraying you. I ended up at the first bar I came across. I almost drank. *Almost.*" I rub down my throat as the burn I always have when I think about drinking courses down into my lungs. "She's my reason. She doesn't make me better, she just gives me a reason to crave a better life for myself."

Edging back to the bench and seating myself there, I stare at the darkening sky. I don't move. The wind whips around my legs and after a while, my cheeks go numb. The bench is my home for the next hour or so as the sun sets and the stars come out. When they do, I stand and stare up into the sky, the stars blur as my eyes moisten.

"I'm not coming back, sweetheart. I know you'd understand. I had to come, to tell you about her. My future is with Laurie. You'll never be forgotten, Amanda. I'll always feel blessed for the time we had. You made me so happy, so damn happy." I feel the trail of warm water hitting my frozen cheeks as my tears descend at the same time as I do, my butt hits the cold bench once again. "I wanted to come and say goodbye. I loved you, Amanda… God, did I love you. But I can't think about the what ifs and what could have been. It's done. Over. You have a legacy, you gave me everything I needed to show me that I was capable of loving someone. To show me I could be happy being with just one woman. Now I know, not only do those things still stand, but I'm happy to give someone my promise of forever, knowing, hoping, this time, it really is forever." My teeth chatter as a whooshing sound pulses in my ears. "I'll always love you, Amanda, but I'm in love with Laurie. You were my first, she's my forever. Goodbye, my star."

Taking one last look at the night sky then back down to the gravestone, I step away from my past and stride toward my future.

Chapter Nineteen

Laurie

This time of the year is always hard. It's been six years tomorrow since the crash. You'd think I would have overcome the emotion that completely encompasses me every year, taking over both body and mind. Ruben is at work. He doesn't know what tomorrow is, or that three days after I'll be just as self-destructive as he used to be. I'm not sure why I didn't tell him. Although I'm fully aware of how the next few days will play out.

Mostly it will include a lot of alcohol, and I'd rather he wasn't around that, or around me. I know he thinks I've been distant the last few days. Hell, he called me out on my behavior, but I couldn't tell him, the words got stuck, burning a ring around my heart.

It was the wall I always had in place, to keep people from getting too close so I couldn't get hurt again. It failed when Amber came along, Sarah worked her way inside and then Ruben just walked right through the blaze. With him, my defense system never stood a chance. Now, I need to keep him away from all my crazy. Plus, a very real part of me is nervous that if he sees me at my worst, he might re-think being with me. The other part wants to keep him away from the temptation, the evil poison I'll be pouring down my throat is the only thing I can think about right now, and that's not healthy.

"Hey girl, you okay?" Sarah asks, sidling up to me, as I stare out of the office window. She knows this day, she knows my routine.

"Yeah, I'm good. I'm going to head off soon," I tell her through the bubbling cesspool that is currently my stomach.

"Mm-hmm," she replies. Her lips pursed. I smile through the tick-toking in my ears.

"Actually, I'm going right now," I choke out, grabbing my purse and not allowing her to respond.

Two hours later and the fog is descending. I've made my trip to the liquor store, picked up three bottles of vodka, which I stashed back home for later, and am now happily sitting at Dutch's Bar. There's a reason I come here every year. The accident happened just outside this place. It singes me on every level by just being here, but I deserve the pain. The self-loathing is something I don't try to push away, not for this anniversary. It's something I deserve, and I welcome every bruise, cut, scrape and tear that the memories evoke in me.

"Hey there," the very deep male voice says, sliding into the seat beside me. I glance up at him, not even trying to feign politeness. Instead, with my face impassive, I turn away bringing my glass back to my lips relishing the burn going down, fighting the nausea coming up.

"You have a name?" annoying man asks. I ignore him, taking another swig, waiting for the darkness to descend. "Hey, I'm talking to you," he says a little louder now and jolts me as he grabs my elbow.

"Don't fucking touch me," I hiss, turning to him, pain slices through my skull as the drink starts taking its desired effect.

"Whoa, sorry, sugar. No harm intended." I glance back at him, and this time, really look into his eyes. I can see the gentleness, and my gut tells me he really wasn't trying to be creepy. I nod toward his general direction, as my eyes seem unable to stay in focus. The pain in my bones from nothing physical finally subsides, as the warmth from the alcohol bathes my senses, helping me forget.

Forcing my body to move, I rise from the stool and make my way to the doors, deciding vodka at home, alone, is the way forward. I ignore the noise, instead making my way into the cold night air. The wind hits my face and my coatless body, making me feel numb on the outside as well as the inside. I pull my feet forward one step at a time, ignoring the lead weights in the bottom of my shoes. My stomach churns as I walk past the point of impact, and I have to force my knees not to buckle as I momentarily lose my footing. I stop and spin toward the wall we hit six years ago, swaying as I go, my rubbery legs turning to stone the minute my eyes focus enough to see the damage to the wall—the blue color from the car paintwork that hasn't ever completely eroded away. The strain hits me, my knees finally give way as the burn comes up my throat. I collapse down to the ground, lifting my hand to touch the wall as the sting of warm tears hit my frozen cheeks.

"I'm sorry." My whisper is as broken and my heart. "I'm sorry."

"Hey," another deep male voice greets me, but this time I know the voice. It makes me close my eyes, the rigid hold I had on my body releases and I slump backward, into his warm body as he kneels behind me.

"How did you know where I was?" I ask, my voice betraying the hold I was desperately trying to keep on myself.

"Sarah," he tells me simply.

What's Left of Me

"Are you mad?" I question. He knows I've been avoiding him, and that I haven't explained why. Shutting him out isn't the best thing to do. I'm well aware of that. Yet, I couldn't seem to open myself completely. We've been together for over eight months. I love him, but I haven't given him the final piece of me. The one piece that I've been scared of giving, the one which might make him leave me and never look back.

"Never," his reply is whispered, and I can't bring myself to ask anything else.

I'm not sure how we get back to Ruben's place. I only vaguely remember him lifting me from the ground. I didn't pass out, but everything from that point until this, seems like a dream, and my brain can't quite put the pieces together.

"Here," Ruben's voice calls from behind me, and I take in where I am. Lying in his bed, I turn over and watch as he walks in through the doorway and places what looks like a cup of coffee on a bedside table. I've stayed over here many times. Ruben has been asking me over and over to move in with him. I've been putting him off, knowing he doesn't know everything, that there may be some things that he can't see past, and this has forced my hand making me choose to keep my own space.

Since Amber left, it's turned back into an empty, emotionless apartment, somewhere I lay my head and keep my belongings. I forgot how empty life is when someone you love leaves. I've been spending more time at Ruben's. The last few weeks, though, because I've been avoiding him, it's turned me into a lonely, broken, depressed woman. I can see now that I should have let him in. Keeping him at arm's length has only made my hurt worse.

"I have to tell you something," I blurt the words out before the churning in my stomach turns into the physical manifestation of all the liquor I've consumed.

"Okay," he says, sitting on the bed and running his hand up my leg until it meets mine. He entwines our fingers, and I look down at our joined hands. Flexing my fingers in his, I try to draw strength from our shared love. Everything we've had over the last eight months has built up to something I never thought possible.

"You've been asking me to move in with you. I want to, truly. You need to know my demons, the ones you said you could see?" He nods. The fingers of my free hand bend until the nails find their way into my palm, biting down and giving me that little bit of pain I need to push myself forward. "The day, in the car, the crash… the one that killed them. It was my fault."

I feel Ruben's hand spasm in mine, and I pull my fingers away from his… needing the space. He doesn't try to take my hand back, and I'm both grateful for him giving me the space I need, and sad that he isn't fighting to keep a hold of me. Swallowing hard as my stomach rolls and I try not to retch, I say the words I haven't told anyone since the cops all those years ago. "I was driving. It was me who crashed. Me who killed the only people in the world that loved me." At that point it's too late, the mixed spirits make an appearance all over his bed, burning my throat on their way up.

Ruben

Laurie shocks the shit out of me. Not because of her revelation, not even when half the contents of her stomach reappear, making the bedroom smell like a bar. She shocks me because I'm scared, I haven't felt like this since I knew I was going to lose Amanda and had no way to control it. This time I'm scared I'm going to lose Laurie, to herself. She needs professional help. Harboring deep and dark secrets, ones that make her blame herself for the death of her family.

"I was driving, I crashed. I swear... *swear Ruben*... I didn't mean to crash. I didn't mean to kill them." She kneels up, her legs lying in the vomit. Resting her hands on my shoulders, her eyes pleading with me, full of fear and pain. "I loved them. I still love them. I was driving, but everything else happened as I said. Mr. Kendall was the passenger, and he did have a heart attack collapsing on my lap. He knocked my leg, effectively pinning my whole body. I couldn't move, it all happened in a matter of seconds, Ruben."

I try grabbing her hand, but just like earlier when she pulled it away, she once again evades my touch. I'm not sure she even realizes what she's doing. It's like both consciously and subconsciously she feels the need to punish herself by not allowing me to soothe her. I know she's partially drunk, but she has to have some semblance of what's happening. Her eyes tell me that she's caught in her own pain, and I need to be the one to help pull her through. "You probably hate me now. I couldn't move in with you, not when you didn't know. I'm a disgusting human being. I killed my family. I'm a curse," she says looking everywhere but at me.

I lean forward and place my hands on either side of her neck, making her face me. Her body immediately calms and her eyes snap up to meet mine. "I love you," I tell her calmly. I let her stare into me, looking past my façade and into my soul, showing her that I'm not lying. Waiting, watching her assess me, my skin heats with worry as it washes over me. Knowing this is my time to be strong for her like she was for me, I pull a breath in through my nose and allow it to pass into my lungs, calming me from the inside out.

"There's nothing you could tell me that would make me run. Do you understand that, Laurie, nothing? Anything that comes our way we will face, and overcome. If this life has taught me one thing, it would be that we will always have obstacles thrown at us. As long as we have the right people to support us, then we will overcome." I watch as the emotion she's so obviously been holding back, pricks her surface and the tears fall, crashing onto my hands, which are still wrapped around her neck. "I'm here, I'm all in. We *will* overcome. That is my promise. If you can't believe in yourself right now. Then please, baby, believe in me. Trust me."

After waiting what feels like hours, she nods and I release the tension that was pushing against my skin. Lifting Laurie up, I take her to the bathroom, sit her down and fill the bath. She doesn't say a word as I remove her clothing, remaining quiet as I strip myself. Even when I lower her into the bath, and get in behind her, she keeps her silence. Pulling her back against me I pick up a sponge and soak it in water, bringing it to her chest and squeezing the water out. I repeat the process over and over, just giving her the peace she needs right now.

"He was such a gorgeous little boy," Laurie whispers and I stop myself from tensing, even though there's a heaviness in my arms. "So smart as well. I remember he came home from school one day, he was so hungry he went immediately to the fridge and pulled out carrot sticks." She's looking straight at me through the mirrored wall I have facing my bath. Even so, it's not me she's seeing as a smile tugs at the corners of her lips. "Now, you may think all young boys are hungry, but he hated carrot sticks, so for him to be eating them, I knew something was up." She swallows and looks away.

I rub my thumbs against the back of her neck, letting her know I'm still here. "We didn't have much money, I've told you this, but Rocco wouldn't feel that not when it came to food. Larissa or more often me would miss meals if we needed to, so that boy wasn't touched with hunger. Still, his packed lunch was never much. A sandwich, banana and a small packet of cookies." More tears slide down her face and she sticks her tongue out, catching them as they fall. Her lip twitch turns into a small smile. "I asked him why he was so hungry." Her eyes find mine again and she bites her lower lip. My heart starts pounding as I wonder what she's going to say. "He said that there was a boy at school, Tomas." She shakes her head looking down.

"Baby," I whisper and she brings her head back up.

"His words were, *'Auntie Laurie, Tomas's momma has gone into the hospital. His big sister is trying to look after them, but they don't have much food. I didn't want Tomas to be hungry. His momma would be sad, and she needs to get better. She can't get better for them if she's feeling sad and worrying.'*

That was my boy, such a big, generous heart. I made sure he took two lunches after that, for the ten days Tomas's mom was in the hospital." Laurie hiccups, a soft smile still on her lip. "He was a beautiful soul," she says.

"Like his auntie," I tell her something she probably doesn't even see. "Do you think about how proud he would be, to know you help other people? That you try and make the world a little better, one person at a time." She shivers in my arms and lays her head back, closing her eyes. "Laurie, you still carry such a heavy burden, one that I don't think you should be blaming yourself for." I feel her body tense against mine, but I power through. "I want you to do something… for you. I want you to consider having professional help."

She opens her eyes and mouth, ready to reply.

"Wait," I demand and she scowls but keeps quiet. I almost laugh at her pouting. "I know money's a problem. I'm offering to pay. I know you won't want that, but listen and I mean *really* listen to me. How are you supposed to move forward with anyone, *with me*, and more than that, how can you run a bereavement class when you can't help yourself? Denial is something you know all about. Let forgiveness be something you learn, baby. Take some of your own advice." My pulse races as I wait for her reply.

She looks at me for long moments but eventually nods. "I want some peace," she whispers.

My lungs expand fully and I let out a satisfied breath. Dropping my head, I rest my lips against her shoulder.

Five days later, we visit the crematorium where Larissa and Rocco's ashes were scattered. The days following Laurie's breakdown and revelation have been hard for her, but she's slowly opening up and telling me all about them. Things I don't think she's ever told anyone. She's also booked in to see someone—a recommendation from Sarah.

"They were scattered here," Laurie says, coming to a stop and turning to face me, our entwined fingers firmly holding one another.

"What about a plaque," I ask, pointing to the remembrance plaques that litter the ground. She just shakes her head sadly, sucking in her lips and trying to bite down the emotion that's threatening. I squeeze her hand, offering my strength.

"We'll fix that," I whisper.

She doesn't reply. Just clings to my hand with a death-like grip.

Pulling her hand from mine, Laurie walks a few steps forward to a small tree, then glances back at me, before facing the tree once again and placing her palm against the trunk. "This is him, Larissa. This is Ruben. He's giving me my future, you know the one that I always dreamed but never dared hope. He's the one who's been bringing me peace for the last eight months. He's the one who holds me when I break. I love him and he loves me. More than that. He's *in love* with *all* of me. Every part. I'm enough…" she whispers the last part and I walk up to her, enveloping her back and wrapping my arms around her chest pinning her to me.

Carefully, I place my hand over hers, connecting us both to the tree. "I'm the one that will do everything he has to do, to make sure Laurie lives a life filled with love, laughter and peace," I tell the small tree.

She brings her hand up and holds my forearm, sending a spark up my body.

"I've got her now," I tell them. Laurie tenses, then quickly relaxes. "I do, baby. I have you now. I'll always have you. You'll never be alone again. Tomorrow you move into my place. I know why you've been putting it off now, but there's nothing between us anymore. This is us living forever."

She nods against my shoulder even though she's looking away, and we stand like that for the next while, watching the last of the setting sun move into darkness. And as the stars come out, I look up and send a silent thank you to Amanda for being my guiding light, and leading me to my forever love.

Epilogue

Laurie

FIVE YEARS LATER

"Come on, we need to go!" I shout through the house, standing at the front door. Ruben walks toward me, Giovanna on his hip. Our youngest, Giovanna Larissa, is such a calm and content baby, especially when she's attached to her daddy. I watch as he puts her in her car seat, and our fourteen month old smacks him lightly on the lips. Looking down at the sparkly bands on my fingers, the physical representation of our love, I think back to our wedding day. Not for one second of the last six years with this man, have I felt anything other than loved and fulfillment.

What's Left of Me

"Rocky!" I shout. Our four-year-old, Luca Rocco–Rocky for short—comes from the kitchen, a milk mustache across his upper lip. "Come on, baby boy, it's Amber's big day," I say, sweeping my son into my arms.

It's just over an hour later, we reach Amber's college. Graduation is everything I'd imagined it would be. People are everywhere, smiles and elation in abundance. I spot Amber with her friends. Standing still, I just watch her. My heart swells with pride as I push down the happiness that's trying to show, by way of tears brimming in my eyes. It's then that I feel Ruben's hand at my back. Letting me know he's there, like always, to hold me when I need it. She must feel us watching as her head turns and she spots me. Without saying anything to her friends, and wearing a full robe, she sprints toward me. As she runs into me, grabbing hold tightly, I realize that if my husband's strong arm wasn't holding me securely she would have knocked me over.

"Laurie," she breathes into my ear.

"Amber! Amber!" Rocky shouts jumping up and down next to me, trying to get to his other favorite person after his daddy and me.

"Hey squirt," Amber says, lifting him up and swinging him around. She puts him down and throws her arms around Ruben. He moves his hand from my back and envelopes her, lifting her off the ground and whispering something in her ear. Whatever he says makes her swipe a tear away. I suck in my breath quickly and fill my lungs, allowing the air to seep out slowly while I contain my emotion.

She then bends down, gazing at a sleeping Giovanna in her stroller. "She gets bigger every time I see her," she says smiling up at me.

"Well, it has been four months since you saw her last," I reply.

"I know. I'll try to visit more often, now I'm going to be working in the ER not too far from you."

Nodding at her, I reply, "Don't forget, the offer is still there, you can move in with Ruben and me. There will always be a room for you at home."

Amber looks between Ruben and me, smiling. "I know, and I love you both for it, but Judd and I want to live together. He's already bought the house. We won't be far from you."

"I know," I tell her as Judd walks up to join us, Danny and Anabel with him. Mandie, Clara and Kyle running around behind in the sunshine.

Over the last five years, our family has extended, beyond anything I could have ever imagined all those years ago when I lost Larissa and Rocco. Now, I not only have a husband and three kids, but I have the boyfriend, probably the future husband of my eldest. I have Danny and Anabel and their three kids, I have Sarah and her family, and I now have a staff of twenty people at the center, all of whom I consider family.

The strides I've been able to make with the center since taking over Derick's job, are solely based on Ruben's help. Not only did he decide that the center would be the charity that his company supported, but he also gave us free marketing. And he called in some favors from other businesses that he works with, showing them the benefit of supporting a local charity. He really has been the rock that he said he would be.

The speaker system comes to life and Amber jumps up. "Oh. I need to go!" she squeaks.

I pull her into another hug. "I'm so proud of you. Amber," I whisper. "But then, I always was." She sniffs as I let her go and we all move to find our seats.

Driving home after the graduation and celebrations, and after saying goodbye to Anabel, Danny, and the clan as they headed home, and leaving Amber behind with Judd to continue the fun, I turn and look at my two little babies sleeping in the back of the car.

"Did you have a good day?" Ruben asks.

I turn my whole body to face my husband. "Yeah," I answer, my muscles relaxing as I lay back in the seat.

He places one hand on my thigh and gently rubs his thumb back and forth. It sends a spark of want up my leg and to my core. Glancing over, he quickly looks at me, his eyes dancing as he smirks.

"You want another baby?" I say half joking.

His thumb doesn't miss a beat when he replies, "Why not. Another version of you, for me to love? I'm never gonna say no to that. As long as you're happy having our babies, I'm happy planting them in you." I gasp as he chuckles, it's deep and dirty, and I know tonight we start trying for baby number three and I'm going to enjoy every minute.

Ruben

ONE YEAR LATER

I'll never get used to holding my new-born child in my arms. Even though this is the third time, it's still just as amazing as the first. Rosina Lily was born only three hours ago. Six weeks and two days after my mom passed. I look over at my sleeping wife and, as usual, my heart beats that little bit faster as my skin prickles with the awareness of her proximity. I'll never be complacent about what life has given to me, what *she* has given to me. After losing so much, it makes me understand the importance of what we do have. Laurie has given me four beautiful children, I include Amber, and thankfully Amber gave me the gift of *her* recently telling me she sees me as the father she always wanted. To say I struggled keeping my emotions locked down would be an understatement, but having both Laurie and Amber bawling with happiness in my arms at the time helped. It's been seven years since we started our journey together, and I'm thankful for every second.

Rosina gurgles in my arms and I look away from my wife and down to my daughter. "Hey, Rosie. Mom's sleeping, you wore her out," I murmur while stroking her soft cheek. My chest swells with both pride and love as I gaze at Rosina, the ache inside my body the good kind. Contentment fills me, and the ache comes from knowing that my world is complete. Rosina closes her eyes again as I take the seat next to the hospital bed.

Laurie's eyes flutter open, and she looks between Rosina and me before settling on me, a smile spread across her face.

"Hey baby," I whisper. "You okay?" She nods her reply, as happy tears gather. Reaching out I grab her hand, careful not to jostle my new daughter too much. "You sure?" I ask again, staring at her.

"I love you, my husband," she tells me softly, warmth spreading across her features.

"And I love you, my forever," I reply, as I always do. Knowing, I'll do everything in my power to make sure this woman has all her happy ever afters.

Acknowledgments

I want to start as always by thanking my husband and daughters and family, for supporting me unconditionally. I love you.

To my Beta's – Beth Lemilliere, Annmarie Thomson, Kerry Adamson, Laura Nelson, Stacey Tester, Donna Tutin, Sarah Queen, Laurie Breitsprecher, Giovanna Bovenzi Cruz, Sharon Dawson, Emma Louise and Morgan Terry. For always being there and just continuously being the best beta's I could ask for. <3

Laura Nelson…what can I say? I just love you. That's it!

To Klaire Sutherland, thank you for helping me with my books. You make me always strive to be better. <3

To Sarah Queen, thank you for being my PA, my supporter, my reader, my bloody amazing friend. I love you, lady! (To your bones.)

Maria Macdonald

To Morgan Terry, thank you for fast becoming one of my inner circle of friends who I now trust 100%... with ALL my words. Love you lady. <3

To Laurie, thank you for sharing your name. Thank you for loving this story. This one is for you. <3

To Maria's Misfits - my Street Team. I never know just how to say thank you in a new and clever way. To be able to explain just how important you all are in my life. When I feel like giving up, hiding, or when it's just too hard (I know we all have those days) you guys are always the ones who remind me why I'd never stop. (Not that I really could even if I threatened to ;-) ha-ha.)

To The BookHookers – A, G, K, L, M & S – (this sounds crazy and it's all the fault of you girls!) I adore you lot, you ALWAYS have my back, I couldn't survive this craziness without you, ladies. Truly. <3

To my Instagram family. Your support knows no bounds. I love you all.

Booksandbandanas
Lovekellankyle
bookobsessedgirl
am_johnson_author
sucker_for_books
pia_bibliophile
beautyandthebooks83

What's Left of Me

naliia_
paperback_pixie
abooklover83
authormandrews
mee_and_my_books
booksare.everything
emmbooks
thereadingruth
bookbarn
doll_face43

To the authors who support me. Thank you. Always

Francessca Webster from Francessca's Romance Reviews, you rock!

Kaylene Osborn from Swish Design & Editing. Thank you for everything!

To every single blogger who always puts time and effort into supporting not just me, but all authors. Thank you. Genuinely… just thank you so much.

Lastly, thank you to all the readers who have taken, and will take a chance on me. You are the ones who will truly make my dreams come true. I do this for you and me. I love you guys. <3

Thank you for reading What's Left of Me.

If you enjoyed it, please consider leaving a review at your point of purchase and on Goodreads. It means a lot to me to hear what you think.

Also, feel free to join my street/reader group:
https://www.facebook.com/groups/mariasmisfits/

Goodreads
Add to your TBR list.
Love Reflection - An Entwined Hearts Novel Book 1
Love Resisted - An Entwined Hearts Novel Book 2
Love Renewed – An Entwined Hearts Novel Book 3
Finally Unbroken – Finally Unbroken Series Book 1

What's Left of Me

Website
http://www.mariamacdonaldauthor.com/

Email
mariamacdonaldauthor@gmail.com

Facebook
https://www.facebook.com/maria.macdonald.71?fref=ts

Goodreads
https://www.goodreads.com/author/show/12764874.Maria_Macdonald?from_search=true

About the Author

Maria is a full-time working mum, she has two beautiful daughters, both of whom love books as much as she.

She has loved writing since she was a little girl.

Reading and loving books, as well as blogging, has inspired her to write and publish.

Maria, her husband, and children now reside in Wiltshire, England.

Made in the USA
Middletown, DE
03 May 2016